The Adventures of Owen Stone

Western Novels

Volume 1

Copyright © 2024 Owen Stone
All rights reserved.

Printed in Great Britain
by Amazon

Index

The Origin of the Legend 4

The Mystery of the Golden Skull 73

Black Crow The Last Flight 118

The Origin of the Legend

Shadows of the Past

Owen pulled the trigger without thinking. The shot rang out, cutting through the air, and the man in front of him fell to the ground, limp. He was barely seventeen years old, and he had already taken a life.

As the cloud of gunpowder cleared, Owen felt his hands shake. He was no outlaw, he was no killer, but in that instant he knew that nothing would ever be the same again.

It all started the night his father was murdered before his eyes, and now, the path he had taken would lead him to face truths he never imagined.

Stone Ranch

The midday sun beat down on the dry dust of the Stone Ranch. Owen, barely sixteen years old, looked out at the horizon as the cows lazily grazed. Ever since he was a child, he had dreamed of leaving this monotonous life behind in search of something greater. His father, Henry Stone, always said that ranch life was the best thing for a man, that the vast open lands were all that was needed. But Owen did not share that vision. Something inside him longed for the freedom and danger of the unknown.

Henry was a respected man, tough but fair. He had worked the land since he was young, and he expected Owen to follow in his footsteps. However, Owen saw ranch life as a prison, a

place where every day was the same grueling routine: feeding cattle, mending fences, and helping with the crops. Still, he respected his father deeply, and he dared not confess his desire to leave.

—Owen! —His father's deep voice echoed from the main house.— I need you to help me with the corral!

Owen sighed and headed toward the corral, wiping the sweat from his brow. His worn leather boots kicked up dust as he walked, and his old wide-brimmed hat shielded him from the relentless sunlight. He came to his father, who was repairing one of the fences. The middle-aged man, strong and weathered by years, did not pause in his work as Owen approached.

— Dad, have you ever thought about leaving the ranch? — Owen asked as he held out the tools his father needed.

Henry paused for a moment, glanced at him, then slammed the hammer into the wood again.

— We've all thought about it at some point, son. But there's no safer place than your home. —She looked at him more deeply. —Why do you ask?

Owen shrugged, dissembling. "I don't know. It's just that… there's a world beyond these lands. Stories of cowboys, outlaws, bounty hunters… Sometimes I wonder what life would be like out there."

hatred was the only thing keeping him alive. The image of his father falling to the ground, the cruel laughter of the outlaw leader, everything was burned into his mind like a fire that never went out.

One day, while practicing with his revolver, Owen realized that he had achieved a level of accuracy he had never imagined. His hand no longer shook, and every shot hit its mark.

"You're ready to face the world now," Cross said, watching him from a distance.

Owen turned to him, a steely look in his eyes. "Not yet. Not until I find the rest of those bastards."

Cross looked at him for a moment, thoughtful. "I know who they are. And I know where you can find them."

Owen's heart raced. This was the opportunity he had been waiting for. The world seemed to stop for a moment as Cross' words repeated in his mind.

"But I warn you," Cross said in a deep voice, "this isn't just a hunt. It's a trap. The men you seek are no mere bandits. They have powerful friends, and if you go after them, you'll be up against something far greater than you imagine."

Owen looked at him firmly, the rage still burning inside him. "I don't care. I won't stop until they pay for what they did."

Cross nodded slowly, but his face grew grim.

and rage inside him was greater than any warning. He walked over to his father's body, tears finally streaming down his face as the weight of reality crushed him. But those tears didn't last long. The pain soon turned to a cold, bitter resolve.

With the help of the mysterious stranger, whom he eventually came to know as Samuel Cross, they buried Henry on a small hill behind the ranch, next to his mother's grave. But Owen didn't let grief stop him. No. In his mind, there was only one goal: to learn everything necessary to bring justice for his father's death.

"Start practicing with this one," Cross said, handing Owen the revolver from one of the dead bandits. It was larger and heavier than Owen expected, but he held it with determination.

Weeks turned into months. Under the relentless tutelage of Samuel Cross, Owen learned how to shoot, how to fight, and how to survive in the harsh environment of the West. Cross taught him everything he knew about tracking enemies, using the landscape to his advantage, and, most importantly, how to stay calm in the midst of chaos.

"Never let hate cloud your vision, boy," Cross told him over and over. "Hate can make you slow and clumsy. Use that anger, but don't let it control you."

But with each passing day, Owen realized that

Promise of Revenge

The shot Owen was expecting never came. Suddenly, a piercing scream rang out from the darkness, and the outlaw fell to the ground, his eyes wide as his revolver slipped from his limp hand. A fleeting flash followed by the figure of a man on horseback emerging from the shadows, firing accurately at the other fleeing bandits.

Owen stood frozen, not processing what had just happened. The stranger stared at him with dark, piercing eyes. He didn't say anything, but his movements spoke for him. Silently, he began to gather up the fallen men's weapons and stowed them on his horse.

"This isn't a safe place for you, boy," he finally said, in a deep, gravelly voice. "Do you have somewhere to stay?"

Owen remembered the image of his father's body, motionless on the ground. His whole life had revolved around the ranch, but now that world was destroyed. Hatred bubbled inside him like lava about to explode.

"I'm going to stay here at the ranch," he said through gritted teeth. "And I'm going to make them pay."

The man, seemingly unfazed by Owen's declaration of vengeance, nodded. "If that's what you want, you better learn how to shoot and survive. Revenge isn't for the weak."

Owen knew her words were true, but the pain

Owen ran through the darkness, his heart pounding and tears streaming down his face. Though he didn't know it yet, that night would mark the beginning of his journey into an uncertain future, full of danger and revelation.

As Owen fled into the woods, a horse appeared out of nowhere, blocking his path. The dark figure of the rider leaned over him, aiming a revolver.

— It seems that the boy will not escape so easily —said an unknown voice, pointing his revolver at him, letting out a malicious laugh.

Company," Tom said quietly. "We haven't accepted their offer, and they're determined to take the land by force if necessary."

Henry clenched his fists in fury. "That will not happen. These lands belong to us, and I will not let them be taken from us."

—Listen, Henry, Tom continued, they've already threatened several of the ranchers. Some of them have disappeared. And I hear they're coming for you tomorrow.

Before Henry could respond, a gunshot rang out in the night. Owen felt his heart stop as he watched his father fall to the ground, blood pouring out of his side. In that instant, Owen's world fell apart.

—Dad! —she shouted, running towards him.

Henry, glassy-eyed and barely conscious, grabbed Owen's arm and whispered, "Son... run."

Before Owen could process what was happening, the door was kicked down and several shadowy figures entered. The young man felt fear take hold of him, but he couldn't leave his father.

Suddenly, someone grabbed him by the arm and pushed him towards the back door. It was Tom Barkley.

— Go, Owen! Run! Don't stop until you reach the forest.

Still hearing more gunshots behind him,

Henry put down his tools and crossed his arms, studying his son with a stern look.

— The West is dangerous, Owen. I've seen too much bloodshed and too many families broken because of the life you so idealize. Here, at least, you have stability. Security.

Owen looked down, but inside the feeling of unease grew stronger. He knew his destiny was not between fences and cattle, although he did not yet know how to face that truth.

That same night, Owen couldn't sleep. From his bed, he listened to the soft sounds of the night: the wind rustling the branches of the trees, the rustling of the animals in the barn. Suddenly, a different noise broke the stillness. Someone was knocking on the front door.

He quietly made his way down the stairs, his footsteps muffled on the wooden floor. His father was still awake, his expression worried. Without saying anything, Henry grabbed his rifle and walked over to the door. He opened it just a crack and heard a whispering voice on the other side.

— Henry... I need to talk to you. —It was the voice of Tom Barkley, a neighboring rancher.

Something was wrong. Owen hid behind the wall, watching with his heart pounding in his ears. His father opened the door fully, letting in Tom, whose face was tense and sweaty.

"It's about the agreement with the Mining

As Owen picked up his revolver and prepared to leave, Cross gave him one last warning.

—Then prepare yourself, boy. Because once you enter that world, there will be no turning back.

Justice at Dusk

The sun had barely set, leaving a red haze over the dense forest. Owen and Samuel Cross moved stealthily through the trees, their long shadows cast across the leaf-strewn ground. Owen's heart was pounding, each step bringing him closer to vengeance. The camp was just ahead, and the voices of the men who killed his father echoed in the stillness of the forest.

"There they are," Cross murmured, stopping behind a tree. From this distance, they could see the campfire flickering weakly through the branches.

Four men sat around the fire, oblivious, laughing as they passed around a bottle of whiskey and cooked something over the fire. To Owen, the sound of their laughter was a cruel mockery of the pain he had felt that night his father was killed.

"The one with his back turned... he was the one who shot your father," Cross said quietly, nodding. Owen recognized the man. He wore the same worn hat, and his hoarse laugh was impossible to forget. His blood boiled with rage at the sight of him so calm, as if he had no weight on his conscience.

Owen took a deep breath and tightened his grip on the gun. This was his chance. He could feel the tension in the air, he knew he only had one chance to do justice, and he wasn't going to

fail.

"Are you ready for this?" Cross asked, looking at him seriously. In Owen's eyes, Cross saw something different, something colder and more determined.

"I'm ready," Owen replied firmly, without hesitation.

The two of them moved forward silently, sliding their bodies between the trees until they were just a few meters from the camp. The campfire crackled, illuminating the carefree faces of the men, unaware of what was about to happen.

Suddenly, Cross stopped and whispered, "I have a score to settle with those sons of bitches, too. They betrayed me years ago. This is as much yours as it is mine."

Owen nodded. It was time to make them both pay.

Finally, they emerged from the trees. Their footsteps crunched the dry leaves under their boots, and one of the men turned his head, noticing their presence. In a second, everything stopped. The laughter ceased, and all four of them stood up suddenly, their hands within reach of their revolvers.

—Well, well! —said one of the bandits, a burly fellow with a scar on his cheek. —If it isn't old Cross... I thought you were already dead!

Cross stepped forward, his hand on the butt

of his revolver. "Not yet. But you will be."

One of the men, the leader who had killed Henry Stone, smirked, his dark eyes flashing with malice. "And the brat… Look at him, are you here to avenge your daddy, boy? How pathetic."

Owen gritted his teeth, hatred keeping him on his feet. He said nothing. There was nothing to say. There was only one thing to do.

—Are we going to keep talking or settle this like men? —Owen replied, challenging everyone.

The scarred man spat on the ground and reached for his gun. "As you wish, boy. Give my regards to your father."

In the blink of an eye, hands flew to the pistols. The duel had begun.

The sound of gunshots echoed through the air. Owen drew his gun with a speed that surprised him. He fired at the man who had killed his father, aiming directly for his chest. The shot hit him squarely, and the man fell back, his hat flying off his head as his body crumpled to the ground, limp.

Cross, for his part, was like a seasoned wolf. His revolver flashed in his hand and two of the men fell almost simultaneously, their bodies writhing on the ground before falling motionless.

The last bandit, the scarred man, hesitated for a second. The surprise on his face was replaced by fear, and he began to back away, his weapon still shaking in his hand.

— Wait! We can... we can make a deal! —he stammered, his eyes wide.

Owen, without lowering his revolver, walked towards him, his steps firm and sure. The rage still burned in his chest, but it was not blind. This man did not deserve mercy.

-Tell me who ordered my father's death—Owen said in a cold voice, his eyes fixed on the man's terrified face.

"His name is Nathaniel Cobb," the bandit said fearfully.

Before the bandit could react, Owen pulled the trigger once more. The shot rang through the air, and the man fell to the ground, dead before his body hit the dry leaves.

"No deal for killers," Owen replied harshly.

Silence fell over the camp. The only sound was the crackling of the fire and the gentle wind rustling the branches of the trees.

Owen lowered his gun, feeling the weight of what he had just done. Revenge, justice, whatever he had hoped to feel… it was a bitter mix. The hatred had been sated, but there was no peace in his heart. Only emptiness.

Cross walked over and put a hand on his shoulder. "This is just the beginning, kid. The world out there is much bigger than this revenge. You're going to have to learn to live with what you've done today."

Owen nodded silently. He knew Cross was

right. He had kept his promise, but the pain hadn't gone away. And there was still much to learn.

In the distance, a wolf's howl broke the calm. They both looked at each other, alert. Footsteps were heard in the trees. They were not alone. Something or someone was coming towards them.

"Get ready," Cross said, his hand on his gun.

Separated on the Horizon

As Owen and Cross checked their weapons and made sure everything was in order, the sound of hurried footsteps and snapping branches grew ever closer. They both turned quickly, hands on their revolvers, ready for any threat.

— Wait! It's me! — a deep voice was heard from the undergrowth.

It was the neighbor, Tom Barkley, a local farmer who had always been a friend of the Stone family.

—What are you doing here, Tom? —Owen asked, relaxing his grip on his revolver a little.

Tom, his breath coming in gasps, cast a nervous glance in the direction from which he had come. "I saw everything that happened... from the hill. You killed those bastards, but... you're not done. I saw another of their gang in the distance. More men coming. They're going to hunt you down!"

Owen felt a knot in his stomach. He had barely had time to digest what he had just done. The faces of the men he had killed were still fresh in his mind. But there was no time to think about that now. Not when danger still lurked around them.

"We have to go," Cross said urgently, putting away his gun. "If what Tom says is true, we can't stay here another minute."

Owen nodded, feeling the weight of his short life on his shoulders. He knew he had to run, but his mind was still stuck on the faces of the dead, the feel of the gun in his hand, the echo of the gunshots in his ears.

"Owen," Tom said, approaching him with a worried expression. "You must go. Those men aren't going to stop until they find you, boy."

Cross, seeing Owen's condition, placed a firm hand on his shoulder. "Owen, listen to me carefully. This isn't the end. What you've done today... is something you'll have to live with. If you want to survive, you must get far away from here."

Owen looked up, meeting Cross's eyes. There was a mix of sadness and determination in them. Cross had been like a mentor to him, someone who had shared his vengeance. But now, they both knew it was best to part ways. The paths that awaited them were too different.

"It's best we part ways here," Cross said, his voice firm as it was, but still laced with a palpable sadness. "If we stay together, we'll be easy targets. You're young, Owen. You have your whole life ahead of you. Don't let this consume you."

Owen felt a lump in his throat. He was only 17, but he felt like he had lived a full life in these last few days. His father's death, the revenge, the grieving, it had all happened too fast. Now, he

was alone.

"Thanks, Cross," Owen said, his voice breaking.

Cross nodded, looking away toward the horizon. "Take care, kid. We'll meet again, maybe somewhere else."

Tom hurried to Owen and said, "Go south, boy. You could hide at the old river crossing. They're not likely to follow you there. Quick!"

Owen took one last look at Cross, who was walking away in the opposite direction.

—Good luck, Cross! —Owen shouted, hoping his voice would carry through.

Cross raised a hand in farewell, but did not turn around, disappearing into the trees.

Owen felt the weight of loneliness fall upon him like never before. In less than three months, he had lost his father, he had taken revenge, and now, his only friend was gone. All he had left were his own thoughts, and the sound of the wind rustling through the trees.

He adjusted his hat and began walking south, toward the river Tom had told him about. He knew it was best to run, but the darkness of the night and the weight of what he had done haunted him with every step.

As he walked forward, his father's voice echoed in his mind. He remembered the times at the ranch, the lessons he had taught him.

Owen walked, feeling like each step was taking

him further away from the life he had known. The cold wind caressed his face, but he found no comfort in it. His mind kept replaying the moment he pulled the trigger, the moment he saw the life leave the bodies of those men.

Suddenly, he stopped dead in his tracks as he heard the unmistakable sound of galloping hooves in the distance. He turned around, and in the distance, through the trees, he saw several silhouettes approaching on horseback. His heart pounded. They had found him.

A Uniform to Escape

The sound of approaching hooves grew louder, making Owen feel his heart racing with every second. He quickly crouched down in the bushes, a firm hand on the butt of his revolver, watching the silhouettes emerging from between the trees. Were they the men coming for him? He couldn't take any chances. If they caught him, it would be the end of him.

The riders finally appeared in the fading light of dawn. Owen noted the metallic glint of the gold buttons on their jackets and the dark blue gleam of their battle-worn uniforms. They were not bandits. They were Union soldiers.

One of them, a robust man with a serious face weathered by the passage of time, led the group. They stopped a few meters from where Owen was hiding. Despite his situation, he felt a small spark of hope. It might be his only chance to escape from those who were chasing him.

— Get out of there! We know you're in there, kid. We don't have time for games —said the soldier in a loud, authoritative voice.

Owen, still with the adrenaline pumping through his body, slowly stood up, coming out of his hiding place with his hands raised. His eyes met the soldier's. The man looked at him with distrust, but also with curiosity. Owen, covered in dust and sweat, looked much older than he really was.

"What are you doing here, boy?" the soldier asked, keeping one hand near his gun as a precaution.

"I'm… I'm looking for a job," Owen lied in a firm voice, trying to sound convincing.

The soldier looked at him for a moment, his eyes scanning every feature of his face. After what seemed like long seconds of tension, he nodded slightly, but still cautiously.

—How old are you, boy? —he asked sternly.

Owen hesitated for a moment. He knew that if he told the truth, his chance would be gone. He was only 17, and the soldiers would reject him immediately if they knew he was so young. But he desperately needed to get out of the sight of the men who were chasing him.

"I'm 20," Owen replied firmly, not letting his voice waver.

The soldier raised an eyebrow, but did not contradict him. He looked at the revolver in Owen's belt and at the young man's hardened eyes. He looked like someone who had lived longer than his age might suggest.

"Hmm, you don't seem very well suited to military service, but we don't make any demands these days. If you know how to use a gun, you'll be of use to us." The soldier spat on the ground and pointed toward the road. "We're just passing through, recruiting anyone willing to fight for the Union. Are you interested? I can't promise you

anything other than a hard bed and some pay, but you'll be with us. And no questions asked."

This was it. Owen knew that joining the army would be the perfect way to hide, to disappear from the sight of his pursuers. The war was in full swing, and no one was going to pay attention to one more recruit. It was the chance he needed to escape his past, even if only temporarily.

"I'm willing," Owen replied without hesitation.

The soldier looked at him once more with distrust, as if trying to read something deeper into the young man before him. But after a second, he nodded.

—Very well, boy. Ride with us. We are heading to our fort to prepare and then we will set off for the front.

One of the younger soldiers came over and offered Owen a horse. As he mounted it, Owen felt a mixture of relief and fear. He had escaped, but he was heading toward a different kind of danger. The Civil War was relentless, and while he might get lost in the chaos of war, he also knew he was about to face a kind of violence he had never imagined.

The Weight of War

The soldiers were heading for the front, and Owen was quickly adjusting to military life, though he still felt like an outsider amidst the rigid discipline and endless chaos. The Civil War was in full swing, and each march was more grueling than the last, while the ground beneath the horses' hooves became more unstable with each step. The smell of gunpowder and smoke mixed with the scorched earth, creating a stifling atmosphere. Owen watched with a mixture of awe and disdain as the battlefield spread out before him. The stories of heroes and legends he had heard in his youth crumbled under the brutality of reality.

One such night, while the army was stopping at a makeshift camp, Owen met Jeremiah Kane. Kane was a tall, burly man, with a deep scar on his cheek that told of his own battles. The hardness in his gaze made it clear that he had seen too much in his life. Rumor had it that he had been a bounty hunter before joining the army, and the aura of danger that surrounded him made it clear that he was not someone to be taken lightly.

Owen was watching him as he sat by the fire, when Jeremiah came up to him with heavy steps, examining him from top to bottom with calculating eyes. Finally, he stopped in front of him and spoke in a deep, raspy voice.

"So you're the new guy?" Jeremiah growled, his words laden with the experience of a man who had spoken over the roar of gunfire more times than in calm conversation.

"Yes, sir," Owen replied firmly, although anxiety was churning in his stomach.

Jeremiah looked at him with a slow nod, as if he wasn't convinced, but also didn't care enough to challenge the newcomer.

—Good. Don't expect a warm welcome. The war cares little for you.

The following weeks saw harrowing battles. The trenches were filled with mud, blood and fallen bodies. The roar of gunfire and explosions was a constant, mixed with the screams and cries of the men. In the midst of this chaos, Jeremiah became a kind of mentor for Owen, teaching him how to survive in this hell that seemed to have no end.

The first serious engagement Owen participated in alongside Jeremiah was an assault on a heavily fortified enemy position. Fear coursed through his veins, but Jeremiah's imposing presence at his side gave him a sense of security. The veteran was a war machine, moving with a precision and brutality Owen could barely imitate. Yet he too fought with unwavering determination, his body hardened by conflict, but his mind unable to adjust to the brutality of war.

During that battle, Owen and Jeremiah found themselves in the middle of a fierce firefight. The enemies appeared like shadows in the thick smoke, and each shot was a race against fate. Jeremiah shouted orders, pointing his rifle at the enemy.

—Enemies at 3 o'clock! —Jeremiah shouted, his eyes fixed on the impending threat.

Owen, covered in mud and sweat, fired rapidly with his tense but firm muscles. The chaos around him was total, the ground was stained with blood and gunpowder and the sound of bullets passing through the air and screams of pain were constant. War, at that moment, ceased to be a concept and became a vivid nightmare.

Jeremiah, firing with deadly accuracy, watched Owen with a sort of silent approval. "Well done, kid. Don't miss a beat. And make sure you keep your head in place, because this isn't going to stop."

Over time, Owen became more experienced, each battle hardening him further. He learned that war was not a noble conflict, but a cruel game of survival where moral choices were a burden few could afford. Jeremiah's teachings took root in him: sometimes, to survive, you had to do things that twisted your soul.

After months of continuous fighting, his unit was assigned to a new mission. But Owen knew that the end of his time with Jeremiah was near.

Jeremiah, who had become more than a mentor, was being assigned to another company. That farewell was a bitter mix of gratitude and sadness, knowing that the man who had helped him survive the chaos would soon no longer be at his side.

One night before Jeremiah was due to leave, Owen found him sitting by the campfire, cleaning his revolver. Without looking up, Jeremiah spoke to him.

—Remember what I taught you, Owen. War may end, but chaos doesn't go away so easily. You can't always be a hero. Sometimes, all you can do is survive.

Before Owen could respond, an officer rushed in, interrupting the moment. He carried with him an envelope with an official seal. Owen, his heart in his throat, opened the message. Reading the words, his eyes widened: a special order sending him on a personal mission, a quest that could change his life forever.

—Jeremiah... I need your help with this — Owen said.

Jeremiah looked up with a hardened but curious face.

—What the hell are you up to, boy? —he asked, his eyes flashing in the glow of the campfire.

Ghost Hunting

Owen took a deep breath before speaking, his gaze fixed on the dark horizon as if he still couldn't quite come to grips with what he was about to say. With a firm voice, but full of repressed emotions, he began to reveal what was inside that envelope.

—Jeremiah... the mission I've been given is not like the others. —Owen paused, looking his mentor in the eyes. —High command has given me the order to eliminate a Confederate commander... Colonel Nathaniel Cobb.

The name rang out like a shot in the silence. Jeremiah raised an eyebrow, recognizing the name immediately. Cobb was a feared and respected figure on both sides. A calculating, ruthless man, with an almost legendary reputation for his cruelty and merciless tactics. But it wasn't just that that caught Jeremiah's attention, it was the intensity in Owen's voice, as if something much darker was behind this mission.

—Cobb? —Jeremiah repeated in disbelief. —That's a big fish, kid. If our people have decided to take him out, he must be causing a lot of trouble.

Owen nodded, but something in his expression made it clear that hunting Cobb was not just a matter of war.

—It's not just the war, Jeremiah... —Owen

said quietly, his words laden with a much more personal story—. Cobb was the one who ordered my father's death.

Jeremiah stopped cleaning his gun and stared at him. The silence between them grew thick, as if the weight of that revelation had frozen the air. Owen swallowed before continuing.

—Several years ago my father refused to sell the land to Cobb. He wanted to expand his mine in our town, Redstone. My father resisted and Cobb... ordered his death. From then on, I swore that if I ever got the chance... I would kill him.

Jeremiah remained silent, weighing Owen's every word. It was a familiar story, a tragedy as common in those days as bullets and knives. But there was something about the way Owen told it that stirred a bitter memory in the veteran.

"So..." Jeremiah began, after a long moment. "This is more than just a mission from the high command? It's personal."

Owen nodded, his dark eyes burning with a mix of rage and determination. Jeremiah let out a deep sigh, his mind working quickly to analyze the situation.

—Okay, but before you get too hasty, boy, you need to understand something. Going after Cobb isn't like hunting any other officer. This man has eyes and ears in every corner. He won't be easy to get close to, and if he suspects

anything, he'll be gone before you can even aim your gun.

Owen listened to every word, knowing Jeremiah was right. He had heard rumors of Cobb's cunning, a man who never let anyone get too close, always surrounded by loyal soldiers and spies.

"I know," Owen replied, his jaw set, "but I can't pass up this opportunity. We have information from the spies. Cobb is nearby, at a farm south of our positions, supposedly overseeing a clandestine mining operation. If we catch him now, we can not only eliminate him, but also disrupt the resource extraction they're using to fund the war."

Jeremiah rubbed his chin, his mind calculating the risks.

—Do you know if the information is reliable? —he asked, although he already knew the answer.

—It is. The letter says our spies have been following your movements for weeks. Now is the time. If we don't act now, we may not get another chance.

Jeremiah nodded slowly. There was something in Owen's gaze that reminded him of himself in his earlier years. He had seen too much vengeance in the war, and he knew how dangerous the desire to settle personal scores could be. But he also knew that he couldn't stop

Owen, nor would he try. He could only make sure Owen didn't die trying.

—All right, kid. If we're going to do this, we're going to need a plan. Cobb's no fool. We can't just go in head-on. —Jeremiah stood up.

—We need to infiltrate, observe, and wait for the right moment to attack.

Owen nodded, feeling a mix of relief and nervousness. He knew it wouldn't be easy, but with Jeremiah by his side, he at least had a chance.

—Thanks, Jeremiah. I couldn't do it without you.

Jeremiah just nodded, picking up his rifle and adjusting his belt.

"Don't thank me yet, kid." His gaze hardened as he looked toward the horizon. "We still have to survive this."

The next morning Owen and Jeremiah set out south, following the report. The lands around were desolate, scorched by conflict and the passage of armies. The scars of war were visible on every hill, on every fallen tree. The air was heavy, laden with the memory of recent battles.

After several hours, they reached a high point from which they could overlook the farm. From there, they saw the movements of the guards, a small contingent of Confederate soldiers protecting the property. In the distance, a man, tall and authoritative in bearing, calmly surveyed

the land. Owen recognized him instantly. Nathaniel Cobb.

Owen's heart was pounding. This was the first time he had seen the man who had destroyed his life. There he stood, surrounded by armed men, as if he were untouchable. But Owen knew this was his moment. His chance for justice, or revenge, depending on how you looked at it.

Jeremiah, crouched beside her, watched calmly with his trained eyes scrutinizing every detail.

"Okay," Jeremiah whispered, "there you go. But there are too many men. We can't just go down and shoot. We need a distraction."

Before they could continue with the plan, a shot broke the silence.

Both of them quickly crouched down with their hearts pounding. But the gunshot wasn't coming from them.

In the distance, a group of soldiers was hurriedly moving towards the interior of the farm. Something was going on.

"Looks like we're not the only hunters," Jeremiah muttered, his eyes narrowed.

Owen gulped, sensing that something big was about to happen. They weren't alone in this hunt, and the situation had just become a lot more dangerous.

—What do we do now? —Owen asked, his mind working frantically.

—We wait… and prepare. Something tells me this hunt is about to get complicated.

Meeting in the shadows

The shooting was coming from soldiers under Cobb's command, and their presence made it even more difficult to get close to their target.

Owen was restless. With every passing minute he felt like opportunity was slipping through his fingers. Colonel Nathaniel Cobb, the man responsible for his father's death and the destruction of his family, was just a few feet away, protected by his men and the shadows. Anger and a desire for revenge burned in his chest, but he also knew that one wrong move would ruin everything. He couldn't afford to fail.

Jeremiah, always calm, remained focused. His experience had taught him to be patient, to calculate each step before moving forward. He knew the emotional baggage Owen carried with him, but he also understood that revenge could cloud judgment. The plan had to be precise.

The silence between them was broken when Jeremiah pulled out a small bag of dynamite. They had planned to use it to create a distraction, and Jeremiah knew exactly how and when to do it.

"Go around the east side, Owen," Jeremiah said as he adjusted the fuse on the dynamite. "Wait for my signal. When you see the explosion, head straight for the main house. If Cobb is there, that will be your chance. But be careful, kid. This man is dangerous, and he wouldn't

hesitate to kill you if he gets the chance."

Owen swallowed, aware of the risks, and began to move in the darkness. His heartbeat seemed so loud that he feared the soldiers could hear it. He stopped when he reached the edge of the farm, hidden behind an old dead tree. From there, he had a clear view of the main house, where Cobb was reportedly staying.

Jeremiah, for his part, had slipped away in the darkness to a small abandoned cabin, far from the farm. He placed the dynamite at the base of the structure and lit the fuse with firm, quick hands. The faint sound of the crackling was enough to quicken his pulse, but the veteran remained calm. He stepped away, moving quickly to a safe spot.

A few seconds later, the roar of the explosion echoed throughout the valley.

The cabin disintegrated in a cloud of dust and fire, and chaos broke out in the Confederate camp. Shocked and disoriented soldiers began to run toward the source of the explosion. Shouts of orders and confusion filled the air. Just as they had planned, most of the men rushed to investigate the incident, leaving the farmhouse nearly unprotected.

Owen knew this was the moment. With the sound of the explosion still ringing in his ears, he quickly crept towards the main house. The atmosphere was stifling, with a mixture of smoke

and dust filling the air. Shadows danced on the walls of the house as the oil lamps swayed from the shaking caused by the explosion.

There were only two or three soldiers near the house, but they were too distracted by the confusion to notice Owen. With quick, silent movements, he slipped through a side window and into the gloom of the interior.

Owen's heart was pounding as he made his way down the dark hallway of the house. He knew Cobb was nearby, probably in the master bedroom, and each step he took brought him closer to his goal. He passed a table covered in maps and papers, clear signs that Cobb wasn't just overseeing the mine, but was planning something much bigger.

Owen finally reached the door of a room, and his breathing quickened. He paused for a moment, resting his hand on the rough wood of the door, trying to calm himself. He knew that on the other side was the man who had marked his life with blood. The man who had destroyed everything he loved.

He pushed the door gently.

Inside, sitting on a wooden chair with a glass of whiskey in his hand, was Nathaniel Cobb. Dressed in his Confederate officer's uniform, Cobb appeared relaxed, oblivious to the chaos that had broken out outside. His cold, dark eyes rested on Owen with a mixture of surprise and

mockery.

—Who the hell are you? —Cobb asked, in a deep, defiant voice, without getting up from his seat.

Owen, his hand shaking, pointed his pistol straight at Cobb's heart. The colonel looked at him with a lopsided smile, as if the situation didn't bother him in the least.

"Do you really think you can kill me, boy?" Cobb said in a scornful tone. "Who sent you? What do you hope to gain from this?"

Owen stepped forward, his eyes filled with anger and pain. He felt the words swirling in his throat, but he wasn't sure if he should speak or just pull the trigger and end it all.

"You..." he said finally, his voice tense. "You killed my father."

Cobb raised an eyebrow, as if searching his memory. Then a cruel smile spread across his face.

—Your father? —he said, with a sarcastic laugh. —Ah, I see. Another insignificant peasant who got in my way. I must have killed many for you to come here seeking revenge.

Owen felt his anger growing with every word that came out of Cobb's mouth. His hands were shaking, but he tried to remain calm.

"My father refused to sell you his lands... and you had him killed." Owen took a step closer. "And now, I have come to bring justice."

Cobb let out a mocking laugh, as if he found the situation pathetic.

"Justice?" he said, raising his glass of whiskey to Owen, as if toasting the irony. "Boy, there is no justice in this life, only power. And I have it all." He leaned forward, his eyes shining in the light. "If you kill one man like me, others will come. And they won't rest until everything you love is destroyed."

Owen pulled the trigger.

But at that moment, the door was flung open and a soldier burst into the room.

— Colonel Cobb! —the soldier shouted. — We have a problem!

The bullet embedded itself in the wall next to Cobb's head. The colonel rose from his chair, throwing the glass of whiskey to the floor in fury.

—Get him! —Cobb ordered, as the footsteps of more soldiers echoed down the hallway.

Owen, heart racing and adrenaline pumping, knew he had to act fast or his time was running out.

An Unexpected Duel

The room filled with the echo of Owen's gunshot. The guard who had burst into the room fell to the ground, his heavy body collapsing as blood began to spread beneath him. The air smelled of gunpowder, sweat, and violence. Owen breathed heavily, his pulse racing like a drum beating incessantly in his chest. Outside, gunshots echoed in the distance, the familiar sound of combat telling Owen that Jeremiah was fighting for his life. There was no time to hesitate.

Owen turned to Cobb, who was now standing, his eyes cold and calculating. The colonel was not a man to be easily intimidated, and although Owen's previous shot had missed, Cobb remained calm, assessing the situation with the gaze of a man accustomed to coming out on top.

"Put your holster on, Cobb," Owen growled, his voice filled with suppressed rage. "We're going to do this right. A duel… you and me. Man to man."

Cobb looked at him for a few seconds and despite the tension in the atmosphere, his sarcasm stood out.

— A duel? — Cobb gave a short laugh. — Is that how you want to settle this, boy? — His eyes flashed with a cruel glint. — Very well, I will grant you that wish.

The colonel bent down to pick up his holster and revolver from a nearby table. As he strapped it to his hip, Owen kept his eyes on him. He knew Cobb was a fast and dangerous man, not just a commander who just gave orders from the rear. He was a seasoned soldier, someone who had survived more duels and battles than Owen could imagine. This confrontation would not be easy.

Owen, fingers close to his revolver, took a deep breath, calming the trembling in his hands. Outside, Jeremiah's gunfire continued, and for a brief second, Owen feared his friend wouldn't make it. But in that moment, he could only focus on the man in front of him. Nathaniel Cobb, his father's killer. Everything he had felt for years, all the anger, the pain, and the desire for revenge, was converging in this moment.

"Let's go outside," Owen said, pointing toward the door. Duels weren't fought in closed rooms. This one had to be fair, fair, even if deep inside he knew there was nothing fair about facing a man as ruthless as Cobb.

The colonel said nothing more. With eerie calm, he walked to the door and out into the open air. Owen followed close behind, the chill of the night biting at his skin. The farmhouse was bathed in moonlight, and in the distance, the flames from the explosion Jeremiah had set still flickered, lighting up the horizon like a hellfire.

They stopped in the center of the clearing, about fifteen meters away from each other. The silence around them seemed almost unreal, broken only by the sporadic gunfire in the distance and the sound of their breathing.

Cobb didn't seem worried about what was about to happen. He was sure he would win. He had survived too many battles to fear a young man seeking revenge.

For a brief moment, time seemed to stand still. The entire world shrank to those few meters away, to the hands resting next to the revolvers. The wind whispered through the trees, as if nature itself held its breath, waiting for the outcome.

And then, as if an invisible signal had pushed them, they both looked at each other at the same time.

Owen's eyes met Cobb's in a split second, but it was enough for his anger to guide him. He drew his revolver with lightning speed, and time seemed to slow down as he took precise aim. He knew he only had one chance.

Cobb had drawn his gun as well, but Owen was quicker. He pulled the trigger, and the sound of the shot shattered the stillness of the night. The recoil of the gun shook his hand, but he didn't take his eyes off his target.

The bullet struck Cobb in the chest, right in the heart. The colonel stopped dead, his body

reeling from the impact. For a moment, he didn't seem to understand what had just happened. His hands, still gripping the revolver, slowly fell to his sides. A trickle of blood trickled down the corner of his lips.

"This... isn't over," Cobb muttered, a cruel smile on his face, before collapsing fatally.

The Sacrifice of Jeremiah

Owen was still standing, staring at the lifeless body of Nathaniel Cobb, when he heard the frantic sound of approaching boots. The echo of gunfire echoed through the farmhouse, and he turned to see Jeremiah appear from the darkness, covered in dust and with a look of pure determination on his face. He was being hunted.

— Get ready! —Jeremiah shouted as he ran towards Owen. —There are too many of them!

Owen, though still dazed from the duel that had just ended, reacted quickly. He moved toward an old wooden structure at the edge of the farm, a sort of half-ruined barn that offered some cover. Jeremiah reached him just seconds later, his breathing ragged, and they both barricaded themselves behind the wooden boards that creaked under the weight of the wind and the strain.

The Confederate soldiers who had been following Jeremiah soon appeared, their shadows cast in the moonlight. There were at least a dozen of them, and they were clearly furious. Shots began to ricochet off the wood, and Owen and Jeremiah immediately responded, firing back at them with a hail of bullets.

— Damn it! There are too many of them! — Owen shouted as he fired from behind a beam. He could feel the weight of the confrontation taking over him again, but this time it wasn't just

his life that was at stake, but Jeremiah's as well.

"Keep firing, kid!" Jeremiah replied, his voice raspy and firm, though fatigue could be heard in his tone. His battle-hardened body was beginning to feel the strain.

The gunfire continued, relentless, and little by little, the Confederate soldiers began to surround Owen and Jeremiah's position. It was only a matter of time before they were outnumbered and outnumbered. In a moment of carelessness, a bullet pierced the thin wooden protection, striking Jeremiah in the side.

Jeremiah let out a stifled groan as he reached to his side, where blood was beginning to soak through his shirt. He stumbled backwards, leaning on a beam as he gritted his teeth in pain. Owen, seeing his friend injured, ran to him, his heart pounding in his chest.

"Jeremiah!" she cried, kneeling beside him. The wound was deep, and though Jeremiah tried to stay upright, it was clear that he was badly hurt.

"Easy there, kid," Jeremiah murmured, his face pale but his gaze still fierce. "It's just another wound. Nothing I haven't handled before."

But they both knew the truth. The blood was coming out fast, and every breath Jeremiah took was becoming labored. As the gunshots continued to ring out around them, the veteran grabbed Owen by the arm, his strength belying his weakened state.

"Listen to me, Owen," Jeremiah said firmly. "This... this is over for me. My time has come." Owen tried to interrupt, but Jeremiah held up his hand. "No. There's no time for that. You know I'm not getting out of this."

"Don't say that," Owen replied, his voice filled with anguish. "I can get you out of here. We can fight together."

But Jeremiah shook his head, a weak smile curving his chapped lips.

"No, kid... I've fought enough. Now it's your turn." He took a deep breath before continuing. "I'll hold them off. You... you have to go. You have something to fight for. Something to live for."

Owen felt desperation begin to take hold. Jeremiah, who had become his mentor, his comrade in arms, was willing to sacrifice himself for him.

"I can't leave you here," Owen insisted, looking at his friend with eyes full of emotion. But Jeremiah squeezed his arm tighter, forcing him to look into his eyes.

—Listen, Owen. My time... is up. But you... —he coughed, spitting up some blood—. You can do more. You can change things. You've learned everything you needed to know. Now... it's time for you to move on.

Owen hesitated, but the soldiers were getting closer. The gunfire was louder, and the sound of

boots on the ground was getting closer. Jeremiah, with a superhuman effort, stood up, staggering a little but staying upright.

—I'm going to distract them and get out of here. —She gave him a serious look. —That's an order.

Owen stared at him for a few long seconds, an internal struggle evident on his face. He knew Jeremiah was right, but the thought of leaving him there, hurt and alone, was heartbreaking. Finally, with a lump in his throat, he nodded slowly.

"I won't forget you, Jeremiah," Owen murmured, knowing those would probably be the last words she would say to him.

Jeremiah smiled a tired but proud smile.

—I know, kid.

With those words, Jeremiah turned to the soldiers, his eyes filled with steely determination. Limping slightly, he positioned himself behind the sturdiest beam he could find, his revolver loaded and ready for what would be his last fight. Without looking back, he shouted:

— Run, Owen! Don't look back, dammit!

Owen gritted his teeth, his heart torn between the pain of losing his mentor and the need to survive. He knew Jeremiah was willing to die to give him a chance. With one last look at the man who had taught him so much, Owen stood up and ran into the darkness, his mind filled with

confusion and sadness.

Jeremiah stood alone, bullets whizzing past his head. Taking a deep breath, he prepared for his final stand. He aimed carefully, calculating each shot. He took down one of the soldiers who got too close, then another. He knew he couldn't take them all, but he would make them pay dearly for every foot the soldiers advanced.

—Come! —He shouted loudly, his voice echoing in the night—. Here I am, you damned bastards!

The soldiers responded with a hail of gunfire. Jeremiah felt a fresh wave of pain as a bullet hit him in the shoulder, but he didn't stop. With each hit he received, he kept firing, clinging to life just long enough to make sure Owen was safe.

The seconds seemed to drag on forever, and the sound of gunfire became deafening. Jeremiah knew his time was running out. His body was no longer responding as it once had, and blood was flowing more strongly from his wounds. Despite everything, a smile remained on his lips.

"You did it, kid," he muttered to himself. "You did it."

Owen, in the distance, heard the last shots before silence ruled the night. He knew what it meant, but he couldn't stop himself. Jeremiah's sacrifice had given him a chance to live, and he had to honor that decision.

Memories of a Past

It had been months since Jeremiah's death and Cobb's fall, but the emptiness in Owen's chest remained. The battles he'd fought since that day had scarred him in ways he still couldn't fully understand. Each new engagement in the civil war had been a test of his soul. The line between good and evil, once so clear, was now so blurred he wondered if it even existed at all. Men fell for empty causes, while entire towns were reduced to ashes, victims of greed and ambition. War was nothing more than a spiral of destruction.

The memory of Jeremiah kept coming back to her. In her dreams, she saw him as he had been in his final moments, mortally wounded but serene. She remembered his words: "My time… is up." They had echoed in her heart like a sentence, reminding her that war would never bring her the justice she had sought since Cobb had taken her father from her. The fight for redemption was not fought on battlefields, and the weight of so many pointless deaths made her wonder if she would ever find peace.

On a cold spring morning in 1865, the news came: the war was over. White flags fluttered across the fields, guns fell silent, and exhausted Union and Confederate soldiers alike made peace. Cries of relief and embraces filled the air, but Owen remained silent, watching from a distance. The peace everyone was celebrating

brought no comfort to his mind. He wondered, "What now?" What could a man trained for war, hardened by violence, do in peacetime?

For weeks he wandered aimlessly, moving from town to town. He felt like a ghost in a land he no longer recognized. The glow of victory meant nothing to him. He needed something more, a purpose.

One day, in a dusty saloon near the Mexican border, fate showed him a different path. As he sipped his whiskey, a sign on the wall caught his eye: "Wanted: $500 reward for criminal 'Crow' Callahan. Dead or alive." Owen studied it silently, his fingers tracing the rim of his glass as the thought slowly formed in his mind. Catching a criminal like Callahan meant not only money, but also something he had longed for for so long: justice. Not the abstract justice of the battlefields, but a personal justice, the chance to cleanse the evil that plagued the world.

The sound of a chair scraping brought him out of his thoughts. A burly man with a scruffy beard and the look of someone who had seen too much sat down next to him. It was Jesse Morgan, a veteran bounty hunter, known in the Old West for tracking down the most dangerous outlaws.

—Thinking about going into business? — Jesse asked, pointing at the sign Owen had been staring at.

Owen looked up. "War taught me how to

fight, but it didn't give me the justice I hoped for. Maybe it's time to try something different." The answer was sincere, filled with the experience of a man who had already lost too much.

Jesse let out a low laugh, though there was no amusement in his eyes. "The life of a bounty hunter is hard, kid. It's not like war. Here, every man you catch leaves you something, corrupts you in some way. The money is good, but the hunt can get personal. And when it does… there's no turning back."

Owen took a long drink, feeling the burn of the whiskey go down his throat. "I will not be corrupted. I'm not here for the money. I'm after something more… justice." He paused, his voice firm as steel, and thought. "What Cobb took from me was never just about land or power. I want to make sure people like him never do that to anyone else again."

Jesse stared at him in silence for a few seconds. Finally, he nodded. "Well, kid, if that's what you're after, you'd better learn from the best."

Owen dropped a few coins on the counter and walked out of the saloon. For the first time in months, he felt like he had a clear purpose. He was going to be a bounty hunter. Not just for the money, but to find his own redemption, to cleanse the Old West of the men who brought chaos and suffering.

Days later, he arrived in a larger town, a place that seemed to have prospered despite the war. Walking through the dusty streets, Owen couldn't help but notice how people avoided his gaze, realizing the presence of a man who didn't belong there. He headed to the sheriff's office, looking for answers.

The sheriff, an elderly man with a stern countenance weathered by years of law and order, greeted him with a questioning look. His badge gleamed in the sun, a reminder that the law had a name and a face here.

"What brings you here, stranger?" the sheriff asked, leaning on his desk.

Owen stood firm in front of him, without hesitation, asking, "What does one have to do to be a bounty hunter?"

The sheriff looked at him carefully, his eyes assessing. "Being a bounty hunter isn't for everyone, boy. You'll have to walk the fine line between law and lawlessness. It's not just about shooting a gun or riding a horse. Catching these men takes more than strength. It takes patience, intelligence, and a keen sense of justice that not many have. Are you sure you're up to something like that?"

Owen kept his gaze locked with the sheriff's eyes, his voice steady. "I've seen the worst of humanity in war. I've lost friends, I've seen greed destroy lives, and I've been on the brink of death

more times than I can count. I know what it's like to deal with the darkness. But I also know that I can do something good, something right. I'm not after the money. I want the men who think they can escape the law to pay for what they've done."

The sheriff looked at him for a long moment before nodding. "Very well. If you're determined, I'll give you some advice. First, know your prey. It's not just about chasing them, it's about understanding them, knowing how they think. Second, always remember that this job will put you to the limit. No matter how righteous you think you are, every outlaw you catch will leave a mark on you, and if you're not careful, justice will be confused with vengeance."

Owen nodded, listening intently. He knew the sheriff was right. This path wouldn't be easy, but it was the only one he felt he could follow. It wasn't just about catching criminals, it was about redeeming his soul in the process.

"I'll put you in touch with some contacts," the sheriff said, pulling a piece of paper from his desk and beginning to write a list. "They're veterans at this, and if you prove to be as serious as you say you are, they'll lead you down the right path."

Owen took the paper and put it in his jacket. "Thanks, Sheriff."

The sheriff looked at him once more before nodding slowly. "Good luck, son. Because if you

fail, this world will swallow you up without mercy."

With those words echoing in his mind, Owen walked out of the sheriff's office. A new chapter in his life had begun:

Bounty hunter.

A New Direction

It had been several months since Owen became a bounty hunter. He had pursued criminals of all kinds: murderers, cattle rustlers, outlaws who had left behind a trail of death and destruction. With each capture, his reputation grew, and his name began to be recognized in the towns of the Old West. Owen was no longer the young, inexperienced soldier who had fought in the war; he was now a hardened man, with a keen instinct to track and hunt his prey.

One afternoon, as he was relaxing in a saloon in a small, dusty town on the edge of the desert, something caught his eye. On the bulletin board hung a sign, slightly wrinkled by the wind. "Wanted: $1000 reward for criminal Luther Carter, kidnapper of Sarah Dempsey. Dead or alive."

The poster detailed that Carter had kidnapped the daughter of a prominent rancher and was believed to be holding her captive somewhere north of town. The reward was high, which meant this was a dangerous case. Owen walked over to the poster and ripped it off the board, folding it carefully and storing it in his leather jacket. He knew this was his chance, not only to make a tidy sum, but to bring justice and save an innocent woman.

After gathering information in the village, he mounted his horse and began following Carter's

trail. The first clues led him down a winding road through the mountains, following the fresh tracks of a horse-drawn wagon. He asked farmers and travelers if they had seen anyone with the outlaw's characteristics. Some confirmed seeing a man matching the description pass by, always accompanied by a young girl who seemed frightened.

The tracks led him into a dense forest, a remote and inhospitable place, far from any settlement. Owen knew he was getting close. The trail led him to a small wooden hut, hidden among the trees. The wind rustled through the branches, and the air was thick and humid, as if the forest itself wanted to warn him that what was coming would not be easy.

Owen dismounted cautiously, making sure he hadn't been seen. From a distance, he watched the shack. A light plume of smoke rose from the roof, a sign that someone was inside. He approached slowly, keeping to the shadows of the trees, and listened to the voices coming from within. It was Luther Carter, talking to someone else, probably the kidnapped girl.

With his revolver drawn, Owen moved stealthily around the shack, looking for a way in undetected. On one side was a broken window, through which he could see the scene. Inside, Luther was standing with his back to the window, while Sarah Dempsey, a young woman

in her twenties, was tied to a chair in the corner, a look of fear and despair on her face.

Owen took a deep breath. He had to act fast and with precision. He couldn't risk Carter hurting the girl. He decided the best way was to lure Carter out of the cabin.

He threw a rock towards the nearby trees, and the noise made the outlaw look up. "Who's there?" Luther shouted, his hand slowly approaching his revolver.

Owen waited for Carter to emerge from the shack before confronting him. As soon as the door creaked open, Owen stepped out of hiding, pointing his pistol directly at the outlaw.

—Luther Carter—, he said in a firm voice.

The outlaw looked at him with contempt and a cruel smile formed on his face. "You have no idea what you're doing. No one catches me. Much less a brat like you."

In a quick movement, Carter tried to draw his weapon, but Owen was already prepared. With a well-aimed shot, he knocked down the kidnapper, who fell to the ground, fatally.

Silence returned to the forest, broken only by the sound of birds and the wind in the trees. Owen put away his revolver and headed toward the hut. Sarah was still tied up, tears in her eyes but with a look of relief that her captor had been arrested.

"You're safe," Owen told her as he untied her.

"It's all over."

Sarah looked at him with her green eyes filled with gratitude and emotion. "Thank you. I thought I would never get out of here alive."

Owen smiled slightly at her, although sadness still weighed on his heart from everything he had experienced in the last few months. "You have nothing to thank me for. I just did what I had to do."

As he helped her out of the cabin and onto his horse, Owen couldn't help but notice how beautiful she was. Her long brown hair fell in soft waves over her shoulders, and her gaze, despite having been through so much suffering, held a warmth that surprised him. Throughout his time as a bounty hunter, he had learned not to get emotionally involved, not to let empathy get the better of him. But something about Sarah captivated him in a way he hadn't experienced before.

In the days that followed, as he drove her back home, Owen and Sarah talked about everything: the war, the injustices they had both witnessed, and their dreams for the future.

Each conversation made Owen feel a deeper connection with her, something he hadn't felt in a long time. The time they spent together gave them time to get to know each other, and before he knew it, something was born between them.

When they finally arrived at the Dempsey

family ranch, Sarah took his hand and stared at him.

—Owen, I don't know how to thank you for everything you've done for me—, she said quietly.

He squeezed her hand gently. "You don't need to thank me. But…" he paused, undecided for the first time in a long time, "I'd like to see you again."

Sarah's eyes sparkled with a mixture of excitement and shyness. "I'd like to see you, too."

The Rebirth of Owen

It had been six months since Owen rescued Sarah Dempsey from her kidnapper in that cabin in the woods. From that moment on, their lives had changed in ways neither of them could have imagined. Owen, a bounty hunter who had left behind a life of violence and death, had finally found something more: a reason to keep going, something to fight for, someone to love.

In the months that followed, Owen and Sarah began a life together on the Dempsey ranch, where her parents welcomed him with open arms. Each day, Owen's routine became more different from what his life had once been. Mornings began early, but there was no need to stay alert, to always have his hand near his gun. Instead of hunting outlaws, Owen spent his days helping out around the ranch—feeding cattle, mending fences, and working the land. It was a simple life, but it was also the life he'd always wanted, one that offered him peace and a sense of belonging he hadn't felt since he was with his father.

One fall morning, as the sun was just rising over the horizon, Owen stepped out onto the porch of the main house with a cup of coffee in his hand. The air was cool and crisp, filling his lungs with renewed vitality. In the distance, he could see Sarah, strolling through the flower garden she had planted. Her golden hair gleamed

in the sunlight, and for a moment, Owen stood still, gazing at her, as if he wanted to capture this moment forever.

Six months had been enough for Owen to leave his old life behind. He had sold his weapons, even the old revolver he always carried with him. With Sarah he felt he could leave behind the ghosts of his past, the deaths and the blood that stained his hands.

On that particular day, Sarah noticed Owen's gaze and smiled at him from the garden.

—Owen! —she called with a soft laugh—. What are you doing there, all pensive?

He approached slowly, smiling. "I was just looking at you. I was thinking how lucky I am to have found you," he said sincerely, gently hugging her waist.

She laughed again, leaning in to kiss him. "And I'm lucky you saved me. I'll never stop thanking you for that."

They spent the afternoon together, working on the ranch and sharing daily chores. Owen knew the time had come to take the next step. He had been thinking about it for weeks, and he was more determined than ever.

After dinner, under the starry sky, Owen took Sarah to a clearing near the ranch.

I've been thinking about us a lot. I've never been as happy as I am right now. With you, I feel like I've finally found what I've always been

looking for.

Sarah looked at him tenderly, her eyes reflecting the stars. "Me too, Owen. I never imagined I could be this happy."

Owen took a deep breath and, taking a small box out of his pocket, knelt in front of her. "I want to spend the rest of my life with you. I want us to build a home, a future together. Sarah, will you marry me?"

Time seemed to stand still. Sarah looked at him, surprised and excited, tears of happiness welling up in her eyes. Without hesitation, she nodded, and with a radiant smile, she said, "Yes, Owen. Yes, I will marry you!"

Owen slid the ring onto her finger, feeling a surge of relief and happiness that nearly overwhelmed him. He kissed her, and in that moment, everything in his life seemed to be in the right place. The dark days of his past were just a distant echo. Now he had a future worth building.

A New Life, New Plans

Over the next few weeks, Owen and Sarah began planning their wedding. The land around the ranch seemed like the perfect place to start their new life together. Owen had even started looking for a piece of land nearby to buy, where they could build their own home. He had no interest in the life of a bounty hunter anymore; his heart was on the ranch, with Sarah.

One day, as they walked through the fields, Sarah told him about children. "I've always dreamed of a big family," she confessed, smiling softly as they walked through the pastures. "What do you think, Owen? Would you like to have children?"

He looked at her, feeling a warmth in his chest that he hadn't experienced before. "I'd love that, Sarah."

The happiness they shared was palpable, and Owen began to feel, for the first time in years, that fate was finally smiling on him.

However, fate has cruel ways of reminding us that peace never lasts forever. One evening, after a quiet afternoon on the ranch, Owen returned home from checking on the cattle. The moon had already risen in the sky, and the main house was illuminated with a warm light. But as he approached, something struck him as odd. The front door was ajar, and the silence emanating from the house was eerie.

Heart racing, Owen entered, calling out for Sarah. There was no answer.

The sound of a chair overturned in the living room chilled his blood. He ran into the living room, and what he saw paralyzed him.

Sarah lay on the ground, her body motionless and covered in blood. Horror hit him like a punch to the stomach, knocking the breath out of him. He knelt beside her, lifting her body into

his arms, his hands shaking as he desperately tried to find any sign of life.

But it was too late.

Sarah had been murdered.

The pain in Owen's chest was excruciating, a mix of anger, sadness, and despair. He looked up and saw something that made him freeze: a message, written in blood on the wall. He could barely make out the words through the fog in his mind, but he understood them: "This isn't over."

Owen's past had come back to haunt him. The bounty hunter he had ceased to be, he now found himself on the brink of violence once again, driven by the greatest tragedy he had ever imagined.

The peace he had found with Sarah had vanished in an instant. And as grief engulfed him, he had to find the killer, and this time, there would be no mercy.

The Shadow of the Past

Owen was in a state of despair and rage after Sarah's death. He had spent weeks searching for the killer, tracking down every clue, every rumor that could lead him to the culprit. The life he had started to build, with all his hopes and dreams, had crumbled in an instant of senseless violence. Pain was a constant in his chest, and revenge had become his only reason to keep going.

Sarah's father, Mr. Dempsey, had understood Owen's determination and, though he was consumed by grief, he offered his support. In a touching farewell, he handed Owen his old weapons, knowing that the young man needed every advantage to confront the man who had brought tragedy into their lives.

After months of fruitless searching, a new lead led him to a town, Wreiton, in the heart of the Old West. The town was a place full of rumors and secrets, a fertile ground for information, and Owen entered it in the hope of finding some clue as to the whereabouts of the killer.

He walked the dusty streets, asking questions of people and visiting the saloons and shops of the city. Most knew nothing, or did not want to talk, but Owen persisted, with a determination that knew no bounds.

A tired-faced innkeeper finally gave him the information he needed: A young stranger was in the village's main hall.

Owen walked into the room with firm steps. Upon entering, the hustle and bustle of the place hit him immediately. Cigar smoke and the smell of alcohol filled the air. Owen scanned the place, looking for the stranger. His gaze stopped on a young man in a corner, alone, with a defiant attitude.

He approached with determination, the ground crunching beneath his boots as he went. The stranger looked up and showed a moment of surprise before sitting up straight.

"It's you, isn't it?" Owen asked, his voice sharp and laden with menace.

The young man tried to maintain his defiant posture, but his hands trembled slightly as he approached his revolver. "I don't know what you're talking about," he replied in a trembling voice, his eyes trying to hide his fear.

—Get up and get out! — Owen shouted without wasting any time. Without another word, the two of them left the room. The air was thick with tension, and the eyes of the customers followed their every move, aware that something important was about to happen.

Night had fallen and the moonlight cast long shadows across the deserted street. Owen and the young man found themselves in an open space, an alley between buildings. The calm before the storm was palpable, the silence broken only by the occasional sound of a

window slamming shut.

Owen stopped a few feet away from the young man with his hands firmly gripping the butt of his revolver. The young man, with a desperate expression, also braced himself with his gaze fixed on Owen.

"I can't let you go," Owen said, his voice tense. "You have to pay for what you did to Sarah."

The young man gulped, his gaze showing growing fear. "You know nothing about me," he said, trying to keep his composure as his hand slowly moved towards his gun.

The duel began with a bang. The young man drew his pistol quickly, and Owen reacted just as quickly. Shots rang out in the night, the echo of the bullets bouncing off the walls of nearby buildings. Owen dodged the first shot with his body moving with agility while the young man fired furiously.

The dry sound of bullets and the smell of gunpowder filled the air, and the tension became almost tangible. Owen moved with precision, his cold, calculated shots, while the young man, nervous and shaking, tried to stay on his feet. Bullets tore through the night, some shots impacting on nearby walls and kicking up fragments of wood and stone.

The young man, in a moment of desperation, made one last effort to bring Owen down. With

a cry of fury, he fired a volley of bullets, but Owen, with a skill acquired through years of experience, dodged most of the shots. Finally, Owen managed to fire a well-aimed shot that caused the young man to fall to the ground and the revolver to fly from his hand.

Owen approached the fallen youth, his footsteps echoing loudly in the silence that followed the duel. The youth, wounded and staggering, looked at Owen with a mixture of despair and hatred.

Owen, his heart pounding, leaned over him. "Why did you kill Sarah?"

The young man, with a look of despair in his eyes, finally revealed the truth. "I am Nathaniel Cobb's son," he said in a broken voice. "You killed my father, and I have taken my revenge."

The revelation hit Owen like a hammer. His past wouldn't leave him alone.

With the young man finally dead and dawn approaching, Owen stood there in the silent night, feeling the weight of his decisions and the uncertain future that awaited him.

The Beginning of a New Life

It had been several weeks since the duel that had marked Owen's life. The emotional scars were deep, but they had also given way to a new clarity in his life. The thirst for revenge had been left behind and now, in its place, a man emerged who sought something more than violence and quick justice: Owen wanted to find answers, to unmask the truth, and to help those who could not defend themselves.

He had heard of a growing town called Gold Valley, a place where opportunities abounded for those who knew how to navigate the shadows of the law. With his experience and sharp investigative mind, he decided that this was where he would start his new life. Owen knew that his talent for tracking criminals could be useful in other ways, and the idea of becoming a private investigator resonated in his mind as the next logical step.

The day Owen arrived in Gold Valley, the town was bustling with activity. Wagons loaded with supplies and people moved through the dusty streets, and the bustle of daily life seemed to absorb everyone into an orderly choreography. Owen walked with his steady stride, his sharp eyes observing the small details that others would miss: the furtive glances, the whispered conversations, the worried faces.

He headed to the local sheriff's office to

register, and upon arrival, he was met by a young man who looked out of place, but whose attitude radiated determination and curiosity. It was Billy Prescot, a young man full of energy, who had heard about Owen and his abilities.

"You're the famous Owen, aren't you?" Billy asked, his eyes shining with admiration. "I hear you're looking to settle down here as a private investigator. I'd like to work with you."

Owen looked him up and down, sizing the boy up. It wasn't often that a young man approached him with such enthusiasm.

There was something about Billy that reminded him of himself when he was younger, before life taught him its hardest lessons.

—And what makes you think you can be useful in this kind of work? —Owen asked, his voice a mixture of disinterest and curiosity.

Billy smiled confidently. "I'm good at observing details and I'm willing to learn. You have the experience, and I have the desire. What do you say?"

Owen couldn't help but feel a spark of connection with the young man. He knew he needed someone to trust, someone to help him navigate this new stage of his life.

"Okay," Owen finally replied. "But I warn you: this job isn't just about asking questions and following leads. Sometimes, you'll have to get your hands dirty, and there isn't always justice at

the end of the day. If you're up for that, we can try."

Billy nodded seriously. "I'm ready. There's no turning back now."

The next few days passed quickly as Owen and Billy settled into Gold Valley. Owen's office, located in a modest cabin near the center of town, was soon filled with maps, reports, and case leads brought in by the townspeople. It wasn't long before his first job came along.

The Mystery of the Golden Skull

Sunrise in Gold Valley

The sun was just rising over the mountains, and the desert was already beginning to simmer in the reddish morning light. The air was thick and hot, and the shadows of the cacti stretched out on the ground, like twisted arms that seemed to want to grab me.

I had spent weeks in that hell, searching for clues about a lost relic, something said to be worth more than all the gold in the area. By now, it seemed more like a ghost story than reality. But Gold Valley rose before me like a vision of fresh water in the middle of nowhere.

It was a small town with only a few wooden houses standing with difficulty. Most of them had crooked facades, and some windows were broken or covered with old rags. The buildings seemed to lean, as if they were preparing to collapse at any moment. There were a couple of horses tied up in front of the hall, and a skinny dog was scratching its fleas by the door. Nothing new in a place like this.

I pushed open the doors to the saloon. The creaking of hinges and the creaking of wood made several heads turn in my direction. The interior was thick with smoke and the stale smell of sweat and cheap alcohol. Tough men with sun-tanned faces sat quietly drinking or playing cards. As soon as I crossed the threshold, the murmuring stopped.

I walked over to the bar and dropped a couple of coins on the counter.

"Whiskey," I said simply.

The waiter, a broad man with a scar across his face, served me in silence. His gaze examined me carefully before he asked:

—What brings you to Gold Valley, stranger?

I picked up the glass and gulped it down. The liquid burned my throat, but I didn't flinch.

"I'm looking for a golden skull," I replied bluntly, thinking it best to get straight to the point. "They say it's worth more than you can count."

The waiter put down the glass he was cleaning and stared at me.

"That skull..." he began to say, but stopped. He looked around, as if he didn't want the others to hear what he had to say. "There are those who believe it is cursed. No one who has tried to find it has had any good luck."

I raised an eyebrow, setting the empty glass down on the counter.

—Do you know who has it?

The man pursed his lips, as if he were about to reply. But at that moment, the doors to the salon burst open. A man rushed in, his breathing ragged and his eyes full of panic. His shirt was open, and sweat was pouring down his forehead.

—The sheriff! —he shouted—. They've killed the sheriff!

The room fell silent. The men at the tables stood up suddenly, knocking their chairs to the floor. Some ran away and others exchanged nervous glances.

I stood up slowly, adjusting the belt where my revolver hung.

—Where did you find him? —I asked, looking at the man who had brought the news.

—Outside his office... he's lying on the floor, with a bullet wound to the chest.

I looked at the waiter, who gave me a heavy look. Something in his eyes told me he knew more than he had let on.

—The skull and the sheriff... —I muttered to myself.

I left the room, following the man who had brought the news. The streets of Gold Valley were deserted, save for a couple of curious people who stuck their heads out of the windows.

Blood in the Sand

The sheriff's body lay in the middle of the dusty street, a red stain spreading across his shirt. The shot had hit him squarely in the chest. All around, the people of Gold Valley gathered in silence, murmuring in fear and curiosity.

I approached slowly, assessing the scene. I had seen a lot of death in my time, but something about the way the sheriff lay there, his face hardened by years of service, told me this was no ordinary murder. I knelt beside the body and examined the wound. It was a clean shot, straight through the heart. Whoever pulled the trigger knew what he was doing.

—Who found it? —I asked without looking up.

A young woman, her face pale and her eyes filled with tears, stepped forward.

"It was me," she said, her voice shaking. "I went out to look for my son... and I saw him there... lying."

I looked at her carefully.

— Did you see anyone nearby? Anything suspicious?

She shook her head, hugging herself.

—No. Just... him.

I stood up, wiping my knees with my hand.

"This isn't just a murder," I said quietly. "Where's the mayor?"

The man appeared almost immediately,

pushing his way through the crowd. He was a large man with a thick moustache and a sour face. He looked me up and down, clearly distrustful of a stranger like me, but the situation left him no choice but to cooperate.

"Let's go to his office," I ordered. "We have a lot to discuss."

We walked down the street under the relentless desert sun with the eyes of the residents of Gold Valley fixed on my back. It wasn't hard to see that this town held many secrets, and the sheriff's death might just be the tip of the iceberg. I had the feeling that something bigger was at play.

When we reached the mayor's office, a small space with walls covered with papers and maps, I sat down at his desk. He did the same, wiping the sweat from his forehead with a handkerchief.

—What do you know about the golden skull? —I asked bluntly.

The mayor swallowed and looked away.

"It's a relic," he said finally. "It belonged to a local tribe and was stolen years ago. Apparently it's been passed from hand to hand among the outlaws of the region. The sheriff was on the trail of it..."

—Do you have any idea who might be behind this? —I insisted, leaning towards him.

The man sighed and nodded.

—There are many rumored names, but one

stands out: Black Jack Malone.

The name hit home. Black Jack Malone, a bandit known for his cruelty and greed. If he was behind this, things were much more complicated than he imagined.

I stood up from my chair, one clear idea in my head. There was no time to waste. The golden skull could be the key, and I knew that every step I took brought me closer to the man who had pulled the trigger.

"Thanks for the information," I said, adjusting my hat. "I'll be back when I have more answers."

I left the office with renewed determination. The sun was high, and the heat was scorching, but I wasn't going to stop. The pieces were starting to fall into place, and soon I would discover the whole truth.

First meeting with Billy

I walked slowly through the streets of Gold Valley, dust rising with every step I took. The air was heavy, and the stifling heat only increased my uneasiness. The sheriff's murder, the golden skull, and Black Jack Malone were surely connected in some way, and it was my job to find those loose pieces of the puzzle.

I decided to go back to the place where the body was found. The street was deserted, only the shadows of the buildings stretched out under the scorching sun. I knelt down and began to search the ground. I didn't expect much, but my fingers stumbled upon something hard.

"A single-bullet cartridge," I muttered to myself, examining it.

It was a rare caliber, not something you saw every day around here. That was a clue, albeit a small one, but it indicated that the shooter was not just any outlaw. I put the cartridge in my pocket, standing up with determination. My next stop would be the sheriff's office.

The door was locked, but it was nothing a good push couldn't fix. Inside, the atmosphere was gloomy, with papers strewn across the table and an empty cell at the back. I walked over to the desk and began sorting through some paperwork. I needed something, anything to lead me to Malone or the skull.

Finally, I found a notebook. The last few

pages talked about Black Jack Malone, his movements, and some names I didn't recognize. The sheriff had been close to something big, but someone silenced him before he could investigate further.

Suddenly, I heard a noise behind me. I turned around in a second with my hand near my revolver.

—Who's there? —I said in a firm voice.

A small figure stood in the doorway, almost merging with the shadows. It was a young man, about eighteen years old. His face was dirty and his eyes were full of fear, but also something else... determination.

"My name is Billy," he said at last, his voice breaking. "I used to work for the sheriff. He... taught me how to read and write. He wanted me... to have a better future."

I watched him for a moment, measuring each word he said.

—What are you doing here, Billy? —I asked, relaxing my hand on my gun but not letting my guard down.

"I heard you're investigating his death," she replied. "I want to help. He was like a father to me."

I could see the sincerity in his eyes. There was no lie in his voice, only the desire for justice. I nodded and pointed to a chair.

—Sit down. I want you to tell me everything

you know about Black Jack Malone and if you know anything about a very special piece, a golden skull.

Billy began to speak, hesitantly at first, but gradually his voice grew firmer. He told me about Malone's hideouts, his most loyal henchmen, and how he pulled his strings in the region. But most important was the legend he mentioned about the golden skull: "They say that whoever possesses it will have power over these lands… and over the men who inhabit them."

The pieces were starting to come together in my head. Everything revolved around that damn skull, and Malone seemed ready to kill anyone who stood in his way.

When he finished, I stood up and looked at him seriously.

—Thanks, Billy. You've been a great help to me. But this is dangerous, boy, and I don't want to put you at risk.

Billy stood up with the same determination I'd seen in his eyes from the beginning.

—The sheriff taught me that you don't run from danger when it comes to justice. I want to be with you on this.

I couldn't help but feel a deep respect for the boy. I knew he would need all the help he could get, and Billy, with his knowledge of the terrain and his loyalty to the sheriff, might be more useful than I thought.

"Okay," I said. "But you're going to follow my orders. I don't want to lose any more men on this damned business."

We left the sheriff's office with a plan. Night was beginning to fall, and the desert air was rapidly cooling. As we walked, the crescent moon illuminated our elongated shadows on the dusty earth.

The confrontation with Black Jack Malone was near, and with it, the truth about the golden skull and the past that haunted me like a shadow. There was no turning back. We were ready for whatever was coming, even though we knew the fight would be life or death.

The Outlaws' Refuge

Dusk was turning the sky red as Billy and I made our way north. The horses were moving steadily, but the tension in the air was palpable. According to Billy, beyond the rocky hills was the hideout of Black Jack Malone, the infamous outlaw who had been behind the sheriff's murder. The terrain was becoming increasingly hostile, with boulders jutting out like the fangs of an old, lone wolf.

The wind blew hard, raising clouds of dust that clung to our clothes like a rough blanket. On the horizon, the stars were beginning to twinkle, but the true guide was the moon, which slowly rose, illuminating our path through the vastness of the desert. Despite the beauty of the landscape, my mind was occupied with the danger that awaited us. Malone was no ordinary man. He was said to be merciless, and his band of outlaws shared his cruelty. We would have to be cautious if we wanted to get out of there alive.

After hours of riding, we reached a rise that commanded a privileged view of the terrain. In the distance, barely visible under the cover of darkness, was the glow of a campfire. I stopped and raised a hand, signaling Billy to do the same. We both dismounted silently and tied our horses to the trunk of a nearby tree. From our position, we could hear the laughter of the outlaws, who, oblivious to our presence, relaxed around the

fire, enjoying their momentary respite.

"There it is," Billy whispered, pointing with his shaking hand toward a cave barely visible through the undergrowth. "That's Malone's hiding place."

I scanned the camp carefully. In the light of the flames, I counted about six men, all armed. There weren't as many as I'd imagined, but even so, any direct confrontation would be suicidal. I knew we'd need more than brute force to catch Malone and recover the golden skull.

"Billy, I want you to stay here," I said quietly, unsheathing my knife. "Watch the camp from this position. If you see any unusual movement, give me a signal. I'll try to get closer to the cave."

The boy nodded, but I could see the doubt and worry in his eyes. I patted him on the shoulder, trying to reassure him. I knew this was more than a boy his age should have to deal with, but there was no turning back.

I crept forward in a crouch, using the shadows to cover my movements. Every step had to be precise, every sound controlled. Adrenaline pumped through my veins, sharpening my senses. The laughter of the outlaws rose above the crackling of the fire, oblivious to the presence of the approaching hunter. As I approached, I noticed that the cave was flanked by a pair of guards who, while alert, didn't seem to be paying much attention to their surroundings.

I finally reached the mouth of the cave and paused, listening intently. From within came the echoes of voices, fainter and more distant. Malone must have been inside, believing himself safe, unaware that his end was near.

I took a deep breath and stepped inside, moving with the precision of a feline on the hunt. The cave opened into a large chamber lit by torches driven into the rock walls. There, in the center, was Black Jack Malone, surrounded by his men, sitting in a rickety old chair, a cruel smile adorning his face.

"Who's there?" he roared, rising from his seat quickly, a knife in one hand. His men tensed instantly, drawing their weapons.

I emerged from the shadows with my hands up, trying to show that I wasn't looking for a fight… at least not right away.

"I'm not here to fight, Malone," I said firmly, keeping my tone calm. "I just want answers."

Malone watched me with narrowed eyes, weighing my words with disdain.

—And who the hell are you to demand anything from me? —I asked myself, raising my chin—. You're in my territory.

"Owen Stone," I replied coldly. "And I know you have something that doesn't belong to you. The golden skull."

The name of the relic brought a laugh from Malone, a deep laugh that echoed through the

cave.

—Is that what you're looking for, stranger? —he said, still laughing—. You're in the right place... but I'm sorry to say that you won't get out of here alive.

Before I could react, one of his men lunged at me with a knife. But my reflexes were faster. I drew my revolver and fired in one fluid motion. The sound of the shot echoed through the cave, and the outlaw's body fell heavily to the ground, limp. Immediately, chaos broke out.

The outlaws came at me with the fury of a pack of hungry wolves, and I responded with the precision of a seasoned hunter. Every bullet counted, and every shot found its mark. I knew I was outnumbered, but not outskilled. Yet even for me, the situation was beginning to grow desperate.

Just when it seemed there was no way out, a series of shots rang out from the mouth of the cave. I turned my head and saw Billy firing with a bravery I wouldn't have expected from a boy his age.

—Get back, damn it! —he shouted with a mixture of fear and determination.

His intervention gave me the necessary respite. With one last shot, I cleared the remaining outlaws and saw Malone trying to escape through a back exit. Without a second thought, I followed him.

We emerged from the cave and faced each other in the pale moonlight, the cold desert air cutting into our breaths. Malone glared at me with hatred in his eyes, his hand reaching out to his gun.

"This is the end of you, Malone," I said calmly, pointing my revolver at him.

Malone smiled bitterly, showing his teeth.

"You may kill me, Stone," he replied with a coldness that chilled my blood. "But the golden skull will remain a mystery to you."

I fired before he could say anything else. Malone fell to his knees, dropping his revolver as his life slipped away with his last breath.

I stood there, watching the desert dust envelop him, and felt a mixture of relief and sadness. Another life lost in this cruel desert.

Billy came running to my side, panting, his eyes filled with concern.

—Are you okay, Owen? —she asked, her voice shaking.

I nodded and put the revolver back in its holster.

"Thank you, Billy," I said sincerely. "I couldn't have done it without you."

We returned to the cave, and after a brief search, I found a wooden box well hidden in a dark corner. I carefully opened it, and there it was: the golden skull, wrapped in an old cloth. I picked it up, feeling its weight and something

else… I felt a dark curse that seemed to emanate from it.

"Billy," I said quietly, putting the skull away. "This is just the beginning."

We walked away from the cave as the desert wind blew hard, whispering ancient secrets. I knew the journey was far from over.

Echoes of Justice

Gold Valley greeted us with a different air that morning. News of the confrontation with Black Jack Malone and the recovery of the golden skull had flown like the desert wind, carrying murmurs and speculation around every corner. The inhabitants, accustomed to the tense tranquility of the town, crowded the dusty streets, whispering among themselves as our mounts advanced towards the heart of the city.

She could feel the weight of their gazes, curious and grateful, but also fearful. They knew that although Malone was dead and the relic had been recovered, something darker loomed over Gold Valley. The scars of recent violence still marked the town's facades, and the air seemed heavy with a tension that only the Old West could sustain.

When we reached the mayor's office, a group of men followed us at a safe distance. They were like vultures circling for answers. Billy and I dismounted and entered the small building.

The mayor was waiting for us behind his desk, his face, marked by age and uncertainty, showing a mixture of concern and relief as he saw us enter. His eyes immediately fell on the object Billy was carrying so carefully. The golden skull, still wrapped in the dusty cloth, seemed to emit a strange glow under the dim light of the kerosene lamp flickering on the desk.

"They did it," he said finally, his voice hoarse with disbelief. His gaze rested on the object as if he couldn't believe it was actually there. "They recovered the skull."

With a slow, deliberate gesture, I placed the relic on his desk, the symbolic weight of the object echoing in the room. The silence was palpable.

"Yes," I replied, my voice gravelly, still resonant with the echoes of the battle in the cave. "But the price has been high. The sheriff is dead, and though Malone no longer poses a threat to the town, this isn't over. We've only scratched the surface of something much bigger."

The mayor nodded, understanding my words. Exhaustion was evident on his face. He knew that what had started as a simple confrontation with an outlaw was, in fact, the tip of a much more sinister iceberg. The golden skull was not only an ancient piece of great value, but a symbol, a key that opened doors to dark secrets and deep betrayals.

"The sheriff," he said quietly, as if speaking of the fallen man was to summon his spirit, "was investigating a network of corruption that extends beyond Gold Valley. The golden skull is only the symbol of that dark power that lurks in the shadows. This... this is only the beginning."

I leaned over the desk, my gaze locked on the mayor's eyes. I could feel the urgency of what

was coming, the sensation of being on the edge of a precipice.

"I need to know more," I said, trying to remain calm, even though inside I was seething with a mixture of anxiety and resolve. "Every step I take brings me closer to answers, but also plunges me deeper into danger."

The mayor rose from his chair, sighing deeply. He walked to a small shelf on the wall, from which he pulled out a worn, weathered map. He spread it out on the desk with shaking hands. I moved closer to examine it, while the mayor pointed with a bony finger to a region south of Gold Valley.

"Here," he said in a low voice, almost a reverent whisper. "The Devil's Ranch. It's a place shrouded in legend, a site that many believe to be cursed. But beyond the superstitions, there's something that connects this ranch to the golden skull… and to the network of corruption that the sheriff was investigating. If there are answers to be found, they're there."

The Devil's Ranch. Just mentioning its name seemed to bring with it a gust of cold wind, an echo of unspoken warnings. Surely this wasn't just any place. People spoke of it as if it were an abyss that only desperate or insane men dared approach. But he also knew it was the next step on this journey. And he couldn't turn back.

As I leaned over the map, studying the paths

that would lead us to that place, I felt a mix of excitement and apprehension. I knew that what we would find there would not be easy to face, but there was no other option. Each answer seemed to bring with it new questions, and each step forward brought us closer to the truth… or death.

Billy, who had been watching silently from the corner of the room, stepped forward. His young face was marked by determination, but also by the toughness that only the desert can bestow.

"I'll go with you, Owen," she said firmly, her eyes shining with a mixture of fear and bravery.

I stared at him for a long moment, weighing his words. Billy was brave, more so than many grown men would have been in his place. He had proven himself in the cave, but what awaited us at Devil's Ranch was something different, something far more dangerous.

"Thank you, Billy," I finally said, with a slight smile. "Your help will be invaluable. But I want you to understand that this trip will be much more dangerous than the last one."

The boy nodded without hesitation.

—I know. I'm ready.

His words, so simple and direct, carried with them a gravity that couldn't be ignored. I realized he wasn't the same boy I'd met weeks ago. The West had forged him through fire and lead, and now, like a young wolf learning to hunt, he was

ready to face whatever was necessary.

That evening, we prepared to leave. We checked our weapons, stocked our saddlebags with what we needed for the long journey, and readied our horses. I knew the road to the Devil's Ranch would be arduous, and that once we got there, there would be no guarantee of getting out alive. But I also knew I couldn't stop now. There was something dark lurking in the shadows, something that connected to the golden skull and the legacy of corruption the sheriff had been trying to unravel.

We rode out as the sun began to dip below the horizon, turning the sky a deep red. As we drove away from Gold Valley, I couldn't help but glance back one last time. The town looked peaceful from a distance, but I knew that peace was fragile, and that the future would bring more storms.

Billy rode beside me, silent, but his eyes reflected a determination that matched my own. Together, we headed into the unknown, toward the secrets buried at the Devil's Ranch. Every step brought us closer to the truth, and every challenge that awaited us would only strengthen our resolve.

The journey to justice was not easy, but we knew we could not stop.

The Devil's Ranch

The journey to Devil's Ranch was a test of endurance and spirit. As we entered the wilderness, the terrain became increasingly treacherous. Rocky mountains and deep canyons surrounded us, creating a landscape that seemed to have a life of its own, as if the land was determined to protect the dark secrets it held.

The blazing sun during the day made the journey unbearable, but the nights were worse. Cold winds howled through the rocks, bringing with them whispers that seemed to come from the very depths of the earth. Shadows from the moon cast ghostly shapes that moved among the rocks, and more than once I felt that something was stalking us, invisible but present. Billy felt it too.

"This place is cursed, Owen," she said one night as our campfire crackled. "Do you believe those stories they tell about the Devil's Ranch?"

"I don't believe in curses," I said firmly, though something inside me kept nagging. "But I do believe in men who do terrible things for power. And that's what we should focus on."

The Devil's Ranch, when we finally caught sight of it from the top of a hill, was a natural fortress. It was nestled between high stone walls that looked like they had been carved by the devil himself. All around it, the terrain was rugged, full of canyons and narrow passes, making it an ideal

place for someone to hide. A dry river ran at the edge of the ranch, its dusty bed a reminder that life here was as hard as death.

We stopped on a small rise from where we could look down on the ranch. The main entrance was heavily guarded. Armed men patrolled, their silhouettes visible in the light of the torches burning at the gates. The air was heavy, charged with an almost palpable tension.

"How are we going to get in?" Billy asked quietly, as he watched the scene intently.

"With cunning and patience," I replied, without taking my eyes off the ranch. "We will wait for night. We will slip into the shadows."

That night, when the moon hid behind the clouds and the darkness became complete, I decided it was time to get closer.

We moved stealthily, moving silently between the rocks and using every shadow to our advantage. The guards patrolled intermittently, their erratic movements leaving gaps in their vigilance. Billy and I slipped through a crack in the rocks, feeling the cold stone against our backs, until we found ourselves inside the ranch undetected.

The inside of the ranch was a hive of activity. Torches lit the adobe walls, and the shadows of outlaws and mercenaries danced grotesquely in their light. A few men laughed, drinking by a campfire, while others traded coins and stolen

goods. It was a haven for lawless men, a nest of vipers where life was worth less than a bullet.

We hid behind some barrels, watching carefully. I knew that the leader of this place would be the key to obtaining the answers we sought.

"We have to find the leader," I whispered to Billy, who nodded, his gaze fixed on the hustle and bustle of the ranch.

We moved from one hiding place to another, always on the lookout, always ready to fall back if necessary. Finally, we came to one of the main rooms of the ranch. From the half-open door, I saw a man sitting behind a desk. He was imposing, tough-looking, and wearing finer clothes than the rest of the outlaws. Maps and papers covered his table, and the gleam of a pistol rested near his hand.

"It's probably the one swimming here," I whispered to Billy, my eyes fixed on the man.

We waited for the right moment. The guards watching the room dispersed, and we took the opportunity to slip inside. We crept in quietly, like shadows in the night, until we were close enough. The man looked up, surprised by our appearance, and his eyes narrowed in recognition.

—Who are you? —he demanded, his hand moving towards his gun.

"I'm Owen Stone," I replied, pulling out my

gun and pointing it at him before he could react. "And I want answers."

The man didn't look away, though his hand stopped halfway to his gun. He regarded us with a mixture of fear and defiance.

—The famous detective Stone? —he said, letting a bitter smile cross his face. —Your fame precedes you, Stone. But tell me, what are you looking for here?

—The truth about the golden skull and the web of corruption that extends beyond Gold Valley.

The man laughed a bitter, mirthless laugh.

"The golden skull…" he murmured, a flash of understanding in his eyes. "It's not just a relic, Stone. It's a key. A key to a power few understand."

I frowned, my fingers tightening on the gun.

—What kind of power? —I asked, knowing we were close to a dangerous truth.

"A power that can control people, the lands…" he replied. "Whoever possesses the skull can rule the desert and its inhabitants. But there is more." The man stared at me, his eyes like two dark pools. "Your past, Owen. There is something in your history that is connected to all of this."

The revelation hit me like a bullet. My past… How could I be tied to this web of betrayal and power? Before I could ask any more questions,

the man moved quickly, trying to disarm me. We fired at the same time, and the echo of the gunshots reverberated through the room.

He fell to the ground, while I felt an intense burning in my arm. Billy ran towards me with fear in his eyes.

—Are you okay, Owen? —he asked, examining my wound.

"Yes, Billy," I replied through gritted teeth. "But we have to get out of here. Now."

The gunshots would have alerted the others, and we had no time to waste. We left the room in a hurry, dodging the shadows and slipping back through the crack where we had entered. Within minutes, we were outside, running toward the horses.

We mounted and rode as fast as our mounts would carry us, leaving Devil's Ranch behind. But though we had escaped, the answers we carried with us were only the beginning of a dangerous new phase of the quest. The power of the golden skull, my past intertwined with its history… Everything pointed to a greater enemy, one we hadn't seen yet.

As we drove back to Gold Valley, I knew the real showdown was yet to come.

The Return to Gold Valley

The ride back to Gold Valley was silent, punctuated only by the crunch of our horses' hooves on the dusty ground and the whisper of the wind that seemed to carry with it forgotten secrets of the desert. Although the wound on my arm was not serious, the constant pain kept me alert, a reminder of how close we had come to danger. The night chill gripped us, making every breath a challenge against the freezing desert air.

Billy was at my side, lost in his own thoughts. We both knew that what we had discovered at the Devil's Ranch was just the tip of the iceberg. The silence between us wasn't awkward; it was the kind of silence shared by men who have survived something important, something that changes the course of their lives.

When we finally reached the outskirts of Gold Valley, the first rays of dawn were just beginning to paint the horizon in shades of orange and pink. As we entered the town, curious glances from the locals followed us, mixed with a palpable sense of relief.

The people of Gold Valley were resilient, but they knew danger lurked nearby, and our return meant that at least some of that danger had been discovered.

The mayor was waiting for us in his office, his face reflecting a mixture of anxiety and hope. He seemed to have aged a few years since we last saw

him, as if the weight of recent events had pushed him to the limit.

—What have you found out? —he asked as soon as we entered, without preamble, his eyes searching for any sign of good news.

I took a moment before answering, feeling the weight of what we had discovered. Finally, I looked at the mayor, my face hardened by the revelations we had unearthed.

"There's more at stake than we thought," I said firmly. "The golden skull isn't just a relic. It's a key, a symbol of an ancient, dark power that few understand. And somehow, my own past is connected to all of this."

The mayor fell silent, absorbing every word. The hope that had flashed in his eyes moments before had turned to a darker understanding.

"We need to protect her," I added, feeling a growing urgency. "There are many who covet her, and they will stop at nothing to obtain her."

The mayor nodded resolutely.

"We'll keep it somewhere safe," he promised. "In the meantime, we need to keep digging. There's clearly more at stake here, and we need all the pieces of the puzzle if we're going to understand what we're dealing with."

Billy, who had remained silent until that moment, stepped forward, his eyes shining with a mixture of worry and determination.

—What do we do now, Owen? —she asked,

her voice full of expectation.

I looked at him, knowing there were more battles ahead, both physical and emotional.

"We will rest," I replied firmly. "What we have discovered is only the beginning. There is much more to discover, and we need to be ready for whatever comes next."

That night, as I lay in bed, thoughts swirled through my mind, restless and dark. The pain in my arm paled in comparison to the weight I felt on my chest. My past, the golden skull, and the web of corruption that seemed to stretch far beyond Gold Valley were all part of a complex and dangerous puzzle.

The pieces were starting to fall into place, but each answer only brought more questions. I knew the road to the truth would be long, filled with obstacles and confrontations. But I also knew there was no turning back. We had started something we couldn't stop, and I was determined to keep going, no matter the risks.

Outside, the wind continued to whisper its secrets, as if the desert itself held countless mysteries yet to be revealed. And I, Owen Stone, was ready to face them.

Revelations in the Desert

At dawn, the sun was beginning to turn the sky into shades of gold and pink when I met up with Billy and the mayor.

The tension in the air was palpable, and the exhaustion of the past few days weighed heavily on us. Still, the adrenaline of what we had discovered kept our resolve strong. I spread out on the table some worn documents I had extracted from the Devil's Ranch; each page contained bits of crucial information, but also raised more questions.

"These documents mention a secret location in the desert," I said, pointing to an old map filled with markings and handwritten notes. "A place where the golden skull could unlock something important. We need to go there and find out what it is."

The mayor frowned, his eyes scanning the map as if he could visualize the dangerous possibilities it held. He nodded slowly, processing the gravity of the situation.

"You have my support," he said finally, his voice firm. "But be careful. If what you say is true, you won't be the only ones looking for that place."

I knew Billy would follow me, as he had from the beginning. Our relationship had been forged in the heat of battle and in silent moments of camaraderie, and we trusted each other now. He

was as determined as I was to uncover the truth behind the golden skull.

We prepared for the journey with the meticulousness of men who knew that every mistake could cost them their lives. We checked our weapons, packed our provisions, and made sure we had enough water, for the desert would be unforgiving.

Within hours we were riding west, following the tracks drawn on the old map. The midday sun was beating down, the heat was scorching, and the desert landscape seemed to stretch on forever, with dunes and hills rolling below the horizon.

Each step of our horses raised small clouds of dust, and the silence was only broken by the creaking of saddles and the soft murmur of the wind. Despite the heat and fatigue, we continued onward, knowing that we were close to something big.

When we finally reached a towering rock formation, we stopped. According to the map, that was the place. The rocks formed a natural labyrinth, and the feeling of being watched grew more intense with every second. We dismounted from our horses and began searching, examining every nook and cranny, looking for something that lined up with the clues.

Suddenly, Billy's voice broke the silence.

— Here! —he exclaimed in an excited tone as

he pointed to a small opening in the rock barely visible in the shadows.

I quickly approached, and upon examining the entrance, we discovered that it was a hidden cave, possibly forgotten for centuries. We lit some candles and cautiously entered. The air was cold and damp, in contrast to the heat of the desert outside. As we moved forward, the tunnel expanded into a larger chamber. Our footsteps echoed in the empty space, increasing the tension.

In the center of the chamber, we found a stone pedestal covered in ancient inscriptions, symbols that seemed to be connected to the golden skull. I pulled the skull out of my bag, its golden surface shining under the light of our lamps. Slowly, I placed it on the pedestal.

As soon as it fit perfectly, a deep sound reverberated around us. I felt a slight tremor beneath my feet, and the walls of the cave began to move, revealing a secret passage that had remained sealed for countless years. A gust of cold air emerged from the passage, like a sigh from the past, bringing with it an aura of mystery and danger.

"This is just the beginning," I murmured, my voice barely a whisper in the vastness of the cave. A mix of excitement and fear filled me, knowing that what I was about to discover could change everything. "The truth is there, waiting to be

discovered."

Billy, with a mixture of wonder and anxiety in his eyes, looked at me as if seeking direction. We both knew that although we had come farther than we expected, the real secrets still lay in the darkness beyond the passage. We looked at each other and nodded, aware that we were about to enter uncharted territory, where history, legend and truth were dangerously intertwined.

But there was no turning back. The desert had kept its secrets long enough. Now it was our turn to face them, no matter what.

The Heart of Mystery

The secret passage led us to an underground chamber where a dim, mysterious light seemed to emanate from the very walls. Covered with ancient inscriptions and enigmatic symbols, they told a story lost in time. The air there was heavy, charged with centuries of silence and jealously guarded secrets. As we moved forward, the echo of our footsteps seemed to amplify the feeling that we were witnessing something monumental.

In the center of the chamber, a stone altar rested. Upon it, a number of ancient scrolls and artifacts seemed to be arranged as if awaiting our arrival. Among all these objects, one in particular caught my eye: an ancient journal, its cover worn by time. I carefully picked it up, feeling the weight of history in my hands, and opened it. The pages, fragile and yellowed, contained tight, detailed writing.

The diary belonged to an explorer from ancient times, someone who had found the golden skull centuries ago. As he read aloud, the story became increasingly dark and cryptic.

"This journal mentions a prophecy," I said, my eyes scanning the words with growing disbelief. "The golden skull is a key to an ancient power, but also a curse. Only those with a pure heart can control its power without succumbing to the darkness."

Billy, who until then had been watching

everything in amazement, stepped forward with his eyes full of curiosity and fear.

"What does that mean?" he asked quietly, as if he feared the very walls might hear his question.

"I don't know," I replied, my mind trying to make sense of everything we had discovered. "But it seems that the golden skull and my search for the truth are intertwined in a way that I don't yet fully understand."

As we continued to examine the altar, something caught my eye. In a barely visible corner, we discovered a hidden compartment. With trembling fingers, I opened it and inside we found a series of ancient maps and letters, each one filled with the promise of answers. Among these letters, one in particular paralyzed me. It was impossible... a letter addressed to me, written many years ago.

My hands shook as I picked it up. My heart stopped as I recognized the handwriting. It was my father's handwriting. Questions raced through my mind: How could my father have left a letter for me in this forgotten place?

I began to read it, and with each word, the weight of his message crushed me. In the letter, my father revealed that he had been involved in the search for the golden skull long before his death on our ranch. He had followed the same leads I was now on and had left a trail for me to follow, knowing that I would embark on the

same quest.

"Your destiny is intertwined with the golden skull," the letter said clearly. "Follow the clues and you will discover the truth about our lineage and the power that resides in the skull."

My father's words echoed in my mind like a persistent echo. My search for the truth, which I had until then believed was motivated by justice and revenge, had taken an unexpected and profound turn. Now, I was not only trying to unravel an ancient mystery, but I was also faced with the revelation that my own bloodline was connected to that forbidden power.

I felt an overwhelming mix of hope and despair. I had expected answers, but not this kind of answer. I didn't know if I was getting closer to the truth or if I was heading into an abyss from which I couldn't escape. Billy, who had been silently watching, looked at me with concern, understanding that something had changed.

"Owen, are you okay?" she asked, her tone betraying her growing unease.

"I'm fine," I replied, trying to sound confident, even though deep down I was far from it. "But this... this is bigger than I imagined."

The truth, my lineage, the power of the Golden Skull... everything was intertwined in a web of secrets and prophecies. What had once seemed like a simple quest for justice and

revenge had transformed into something much deeper, something that could change not only my life, but the fate of everything I knew.

I knew I couldn't stop now. My father's letter had added another layer of mystery to my quest, and the path to the truth would be darker and more dangerous than ever. But I wasn't alone. Billy had followed me here, and together, we would go into the shadows, ready to face whatever came next.

The desert held its secrets, but we were ready to discover them, no matter what.

The Outsider's Legacy

The journey back to Gold Valley was a difficult one, not only because of physical exhaustion, but also because of the weight of the revelations and unknowns that still plagued us. The golden skull, the explorer's journal, and my father's letter swirled around in my mind like pieces of a puzzle that was just beginning to take shape. The darkness of the desert seemed to reflect the chaos inside me, a reflection of everything I still didn't understand.

When we reached the village, the news of our return spread like wildfire through dry straw. The faces of the inhabitants showed a mixture of relief and concern. They looked at us expectantly, their eyes full of unasked questions.

—Did they get it? —the mayor asked, his voice shaking slightly, betraying his anxiety.

I nodded, holding up the golden skull and the documents we had recovered.

—We've discovered much, but we also have more questions. The skull is a key to an ancient power, but also a curse. And my own past is intrinsically linked to all of this.

I remembered my father's letter, found on the altar in the cave, marked with a date a few days before my birth. With trembling hands, I opened it and read it aloud, trying to contain the emotion that threatened to overflow.

—"Dear Owen,

If you are reading this, it means you have found the golden skull and are close to the truth. I am not the man you thought you knew, but everything I did was to protect you and this power. The skull is a key, but also a test. Only those with a pure heart can handle its power without succumbing to the darkness.

Our family has been connected to this mystery for generations. The power of the skull can rule people and lands, but it can also bring justice and redemption. It was my destiny to seek out the skull and hide it from those who would use it for evil. Yours, Owen, is to protect it and uncover the truth.

The desert holds secrets, and in its sands lies the fate of our family. Follow the clues, find the truth, and protect Gold Valley. Your path will be difficult, but I trust in your courage and determination.

With love,

Your father."

The words resonated deeply, filling me with a mixture of sadness and determination. Each sentence was a revelation, a call to action. The golden skull was not simply an object of value, but proof of our lineage and our ability to do good. It was a legacy that must be protected.

I looked at Billy and the mayor, finding in their eyes the same determination I felt welling up inside me.

"The golden skull is more than just an object," I said firmly. "It is proof and a legacy. Together, we must protect it and use its power to bring justice and peace to this land."

The mayor nodded, and slowly, the people of Gold Valley came closer, offering their unconditional support. The community, once fractured and full of mistrust, was beginning to unite around a common purpose. We knew we were not alone in this mission.

That night, as the sun set over the desert and the stars began to twinkle in the sky, I felt a peace I hadn't felt in a long time. My search for the truth was far from over, but I had taken a big step toward understanding my past and the power that the golden skull represented.

The desert whispered its ancient secrets, and my heart pounded with the certainty that, step by step, I would uncover the Outsider's true legacy and the truth my father had so fervently protected. As I looked out over the horizon, I knew that though the path would be arduous and fraught with danger, I would not be alone. With my new friends at my side and the golden skull in our hands, we were ready to face any challenge that lay ahead.

The Outsider's legacy was not just a personal destiny, but a collective responsibility that we now carried with pride. And in that moment, as the desert filled with shadows and lights, I

understood that true power lay not in the skull alone, but in the bravery of those who were willing to fight for justice and truth.

The golden skull was kept in a safe in a secret location, a safe that only Billy, the mayor and I knew about. The safety of the relic had become our priority, and the weight of that responsibility fell on our shoulders. We met in the mayor's office, where the atmosphere was tense but determined.

"This is a safe place, but we must be cautious," the mayor said, as he placed the skull in his safe. "The power of the skull will attract those who seek to take advantage of its energy."

Billy nodded, his expression serious. "We can't let it fall into the wrong hands. There are too many people who are interested in what it represents."

"Exactly," I replied, feeling a pang of anxiety. "We must keep it a secret, even from those who might be our allies. We can't risk the news leaking out."

The mayor closed the safe, making sure it was securely locked. "This will be our fortress."

As we talked, my mind wandered to my father's words in the letter. "The skull is proof." What exactly did he mean by that? I had to be prepared to face not only external dangers, but also my own demons.

As the days passed, the atmosphere in Gold

Valley became more unsettling. Rumors of outlaws lurking in the surrounding area began to circulate, and I knew we couldn't just sit back and do nothing. The golden skull was a beacon in the darkness, and there were those who wouldn't hesitate to try to snatch it from us.

One afternoon, while I was browsing the supply store, I came across a suspicious-looking man. His gaze quickly shifted when our eyes met, and his nervous demeanor made me suspicious.

— Everything okay, stranger? — I asked, trying to sound casual.

"Yeah, just... just looking for supplies," he stammered.

It made me feel like there was something more going on behind the facade. I decided we needed to step up our vigilance. I returned to the mayor's office and shared my concerns with him.

"We need to prepare people," I insisted. "If they find out about the skull, there will be chaos. We need to reinforce security and be ready for any eventuality."

The mayor nodded, knowing that Gold Valley's calm was about to be tested. "We'll do whatever it takes."

With a renewed sense of purpose, I called Billy to join us. I knew that together we could face any threat. Gold Valley had been our home, and we would do everything in our power to protect it. The search for truth and justice had only just

begun, and with the golden skull at our side, we were determined to unravel the legacy that bound us together. And we resolved to, for the moment, forget about the skull.

A New Beginning

I decided that Gold Valley would be my home. After everything I had been through, I felt that the town had a special place in my heart.

It would be the center of my discoveries, a refuge where I could protect the golden skull. Besides, I knew there was more to do here than just unravel ancient mysteries.

With the help of the mayor and the support of the townspeople, I opened the doors to my detective office. It was a small room with a window overlooking the main street. I decorated the walls with maps of the territory and some old weapons I had acquired throughout my adventures. But the most important thing was the desk in the center of the room, where I would receive new cases and challenges every day.

Billy became my young assistant, full of energy and determination. Despite his youth, he had a natural instinct for detective work, and I knew that his presence would make every case easier to bear. "We're about to become the best detective team in the West," I said jokingly one morning as we were organizing the office.

—And don't forget your cowboy hat! — Billy exclaimed with a smile, as he adjusted his own.

Black Crow The Last Flight

The symbol of the Raven

The day had started out like any other in Gold Valley. Billy and I were in the office, bored and without much to do. But in our line of work, routine never lasts long.

"Owen, looks like we have a case," Billy said to me, breaking the silence.

I looked up. Billy was frowning as he read a telegram that had just arrived. I knew that if his expression changed like that, it wasn't something simple.

—What's wrong? —I asked, leaning my elbows on the table, attentive to his reaction.

Billy looked up, and the gleam in his eyes warned me that what he was about to tell me was no simple drunken brawl or cattle rustling.

"A man was found dead outside the village," he said grimly. "You need to see him. There's a symbol... branded on his chest."

A kind of chill ran down my spine when I heard those words.

—Tell me what it is... —I murmured, standing up immediately.

Billy nodded and looked at me in shock, as if he didn't want to believe what he was seeing.

—It's a crow, Owen.

My heart raced. It couldn't be. The Crow died years ago. And I personally made sure he was dead. Yet here we were, with a corpse and the symbol that had made one of the most elusive

and brutal criminals in the region famous. Without another word, I grabbed my jacket and hat, ready to leave.

"Let's go look at that body," I said to Billy, as he did the same.

The ride to the crime scene took longer than it should have. Not because of the distance, but because my head kept spinning. The Crow. That name carried with it a shadow I had never been able to shake off. Even though it had been a long time since he last appeared, the fear he instilled in the victims—and in all of us who were chasing him—was still palpable.

When we arrived, a couple of sheriff's deputies were already surrounding the body. I approached cautiously, each step feeling like a slow entrance into a familiar nightmare. There, on the dusty ground, lay the man. I didn't know him, but his identity wasn't what mattered. What really caught my attention was the Raven, etched precisely on his chest. It wasn't improvised; whoever had done it knew exactly what they wanted to convey.

I crouched down, examining the wound more closely. The cut was clean, too perfect to be the work of someone inexperienced. It was as if it had been designed for us to find. There was no doubt that the killer wanted us to see this.

Billy stood beside me, silent, waiting for me to say something. But there wasn't much to say.

"It looks like his job, but it can't be him, right?" Billy finally asked, as if he needed to hear from me that this was all a macabre joke, a coincidence.

"I don't know, Billy," I replied, not taking my eyes off the symbol. "I can't say for sure until we investigate further, but… this isn't a coincidence. This is a message."

I stood up and looked around. Something didn't add up. It was clear that the killer had wanted us to find the body, but why now? And if it really was the Crow, what had brought him back after all these years? I felt the tension building inside me, as if the past was creeping back up to us.

"Owen, come look at this," Billy said, pointing to something carved into a wooden beam near the body.

I walked closer, and saw it immediately. A cryptic message etched into the wood, barely noticeable if you weren't paying attention. I got close enough to read the words:

"I'm not dead."

I felt a knot in my stomach. I could feel the weight of the memories from those years of hunting crushing me. We were convinced that we had finished off The Raven, but now… if these words were true, he had not only survived, but he had returned. And that would not be good.

Billy looked at me, expecting me to know what

to do, but the truth was that for the first time in a long time, I didn't have a clear answer.

I knew we were dealing with something much bigger than we had thought. And worst of all… if The Crow was alive, that meant the horrors we thought buried years ago were about to return. But this time, it could be more deadly.

Shadows in the night

After seeing the body with the Raven marking on its chest and the cryptic message, I couldn't get the idea out of my head that the past was coming back into my life. The Raven, or someone who wanted to imitate him, was back. I had no choice but to follow the trail, and to do that, I needed to know who the man who had been killed in that way was.

Billy and I spent the next few hours investigating the deceased. His name was Thomas Mercer, a man who, as far as we knew, had no obvious motive for being murdered in such a brutal manner. What we did investigate did not turn up anything particularly dark, except for his visits to other towns of which we had few details.

"There's something strange here, Owen," Billy told me, reading from a file the sheriff handed us. "This guy worked at a few big places, but no one seems to know exactly what he did."

I frowned, reading the information. Mercer had been involved in several major projects, mostly in the transportation of minerals and silver, but it was as if he had flown under the radar the whole time, always present but never quite visible.

—Do you think he was into something bigger? —Billy asked, looking up from the paper.

"Could be," I replied, feeling a familiar

uneasiness in my stomach. "Something tells me Mercer wasn't just an ordinary man."

There was something in the air, a feeling that this case was going to take us down a dark path. We decided to continue investigating Mercer's last days in the village, starting with the people he had had contact with. One clue led us to a man named Vincent, an acquaintance of Mercer's who used to meet him at a tavern out of the way in the village, the "Black Claw." I didn't like that name at all.

The tavern was located in a darker part of Gold Valley, where shadows lengthened and words were whispered. As I entered, the smell of stale tobacco and cheap liquor hit me. The few people there eyed us warily as we approached the bar.

"We're looking for a man named Vincent," I said to the innkeeper, a burly fellow with scars on his face who didn't give me a good feeling.

The man looked me up and down, saying nothing, then nodded toward a table in the dark corner of the place. There, a skinny man with a few weeks' worth of beard and a shabby hat was drinking silently.

We approached slowly, and Vincent looked up when we were close enough. His eyes showed a mixture of fear and surprise.

—What do you want? —he asked, his voice hoarse from alcohol and distrust.

"We want to ask you about Thomas Mercer," Billy said, in his direct tone.

Vincent tensed at the sound of that name. There was something bigger at stake, and he knew it.

"I don't know what you're talking about," he tried to deny, looking away.

I sat across from him, staring at him. I knew he had no time for games.

"You know exactly what we're talking about, Vincent. And if you don't help us, things could go badly for you," I said, in a tone that left no room for doubt.

Vincent swallowed and lowered his voice.

—Look, I don't know much. Mercer was involved in something strange. He was talking about powerful people, secrets he didn't want to share... I think he messed with the wrong people.

—Who are those people? —I asked.

Vincent looked at me as if he was considering whether continuing to talk was a good idea. In the end, he decided to do so.

—Those guys... They call themselves "The Shadow," a kind of secret society. They control things from the shadows, no one sees them, but everyone knows they're there. Mercer was close to something, and it seems they didn't want him to talk.

That name, The Shadow, was familiar to me. I had heard rumors about them in the past, but I

could never confirm their existence. If they were involved, things were going to get even more complicated.

Before we could get any more answers, a noise at the door caught our attention. A group of men entered the tavern, and I immediately knew they weren't there to drink.

—We have to get out of here! —Billy exclaimed, standing up instantly.

We stood up from the table as the men approached with menacing steps. Vincent took advantage of the confusion to disappear, as if he knew this was going to happen.

We left the tavern in a hurry, but as soon as we stepped into the back alley, I felt like we had fallen into a trap. The shadows seemed to move on their own, and the sound of footsteps surrounded us.

"Careful, Owen," Billy muttered, pulling out his revolver.

But before we could react, a hooded figure lunged at us from the shadows. I felt the thud of impact as I fell to the ground, rolling and drawing my gun. Billy shouted something, but he was too busy fighting another attacker. Punches and kicks mixed with the echo of gunfire, and everything descended into chaos.

I struggled with all my might, but when I managed to free myself from one of the attackers and looked back at Billy, I saw the worst. A

hooded figure had grabbed him and was dragging him into the shadows.

—Billy! —I screamed, running towards him, but it was too late.

The figure and Billy disappeared into the darkness of the alley. My footsteps echoed against the walls as I tried to reach them, but by the time I reached the end, there was no trace of them. The echo of my own screams was all that remained.

I stood in the dark alley, my heart pounding. Billy had been captured. There was no doubt about it, the Shadow was involved in this and the worst part was that we were just getting started on this case.

The empty tomb

The silence in the alley crushed me as the echoes of my footsteps faded into the night. Billy was gone, and I cursed myself for not being able to stop him. There was no time for regrets; every second I lost could cost him his life. I took a deep breath and forced myself to think clearly.

The first thing I did was to check the area for clues. I found marks on the ground, footprints that indicated he had been dragged. It wasn't much, but it was enough to get me started. I followed the tracks to the edge of town, where they faded into vacant lots. Not surprisingly, they took him out of the reach of curious people.

As I walked, an idea struck me: The Shadow, that secret society Vincent mentioned, had to be behind the kidnapping. Billy had been captured right after we found out about them. If they wanted to shut us up, kidnapping Billy was a clear message. And I had already decided not to let them get away with it.

A few hours of fruitless searching passed until, at dawn, an old man stopped me on the street. His face was covered in wrinkles and his eyes showed fear. In a trembling voice, he told me that he had seen some men dragging someone towards the old cemetery, just outside the village. My heart raced.

The cemetery he was referring to was no ordinary one. It was old, almost abandoned. A

place that was avoided, full of tombstones forgotten by time. And in the middle of all those graves, there was the most sinister one of all: the Raven's grave.

The Raven. His name wouldn't leave me alone. I'd already seen the symbol on Mercer's chest, and now I was heading to where his remains were supposedly resting. If this wasn't a sign that something was wrong, I don't know what was.

The cemetery was a place forgotten by time. The creaking of dry branches under my boots and the whistling of the wind between the cracked tombstones were the only sounds that broke the silence. Raven's grave was at the bottom of a sloping hill, surrounded by twisted trees whose branches stretched towards the sky as if they wanted to escape from something evil.

My steps led me straight to the Raven's gravestone. It was different from the others. It wasn't overgrown, nor did it look like time had passed over it. The Raven symbol, carved in stone, glowed in the dim light of dawn. The same raven I had seen engraved on Mercer's chest.

I swallowed hard and felt a chill run down my spine. There was only one way to know the truth. I dug the shovel into the ground and began to dig. The sound of the shovel hitting the ground was fast, desperate. With each shovelful, sweat ran down my forehead, and the weight of

uncertainty became more and more crushing. "What will I find here?" I asked myself, over and over again.

It was several minutes before the shovel made contact with the coffin. My breathing became erratic and the air around me seemed thicker, as if the cemetery itself knew what I was about to discover.

I knelt at the edge of the hole and pulled at the lid. The crack of breaking wood echoed through the empty graveyard, a sort of macabre welcome to what was to come. I slowly opened it, prepared for the worst.

But when the lid fell to the ground, the coffin was empty.

The shock of that revelation paralyzed me for a few seconds that seemed like an eternity. The Raven... the man who was supposedly buried here, was gone. The rumors, the legends, everything I had believed until now, was crumbling like a house of cards before my eyes. My mind tried to process what I was seeing, but the shock was too much.

Was the Raven alive? If so, it meant that all this time he had been playing with us, with Billy, with me... How many times had he been nearby, watching us, waiting for the perfect moment to strike?

Suddenly, I felt something crunch under my foot. I looked down and saw a brown envelope,

aged and wrinkled, half buried among leaves and disturbed earth. I picked it up with shaking hands and carefully opened it. Inside was a single sheet of paper, with letters cut out from various newspapers, forming a message:

"If you keep investigating, Billy will die."

The threat was clear, direct, and brutal. I stared at it, my heart pounding in my ears. Reality hit me like a punch to the stomach. They had Billy, and now they knew I was nearby. This note was no casual warning; it was a promise of death.

Questions were racing through my mind. Why was all this happening? What did this empty tomb mean? They knew I was behind them, but what really terrified me was that maybe they had been waiting for me. What if all this had been planned for a long time?

I stuffed the note into my pocket, clenching my fists tightly. The cold grew more intense and the wind whipped up dust in swirls that danced between the headstones of this forgotten cemetery. Billy was in danger, and the only lead I had led me to a ghost.

I looked around, feeling like something or someone was watching me from the shadows, but I saw no one. The figures on the tombstones grew longer in the early sunlight, creating an even more sinister effect. I couldn't afford to fail. I knew that if I made the wrong decision, Billy wouldn't make it out of this alive.

I walked towards the entrance of the cemetery, but my mind was constantly on alert. Every sound, every shadow seemed like a threat. The situation had changed drastically. If the Raven was still alive, then he was playing with me, and he was leading me where he wanted.

As I walked out of the cemetery, I tried to think of the next step. Where to look next? My priority was Billy, but I couldn't ignore what I had just discovered: the Raven was closer than we had ever imagined. If all this was true, I was in the clutches of a criminal who had managed to cheat death.

There was no time for theories, only action. The clock was ticking, and with every passing second, Billy was getting closer to his end.

A new threat

The air felt thick, like a mixture of dust and fear that burned my lungs with every breath. Billy was somewhere nearby, I felt it. But I had to find him.

My mind was racing as I thought about the latest leads I had followed. I recalled a conversation with one of the informants at the bar where we used to meet. A guy who had mentioned something about suspicious movements in an old warehouse, a place known to be a meeting point for illicit activities.

It was a hunch, but I had no time to hesitate. I couldn't let fear stop me. With my heart pounding, I pulled out my revolver, made sure it was loaded, and headed toward the warehouse, knowing that every second counted.

The path to the place was filled with shadows. Night had fallen quickly, and the silence was deafening. The warehouse stood like a dark monolith before me, and as I approached, the air grew heavier, more tense.

The windows were broken and the walls stained with moisture. From the outside, it looked like nothing more than another forgotten vestige of a past, but inside, I knew something far more sinister awaited me.

With the gun firmly held in my right hand, I slowly pushed open the front door. The creaking of the hinges echoed in the silence of the place,

and my body tensed, prepared for whatever I might find. Darkness enveloped me, but my eyes, adapted to the dim light, searched for any movement, any shadow.

Not even ten seconds had passed when I came across the first one: a burly man, with a scarred face and a cold expression. He was standing a few meters away, as if he knew that sooner or later we would cross paths.

There were no words, just an exchange of glances that made it clear that one of us was not going to get out of there unscathed. Without time to think, I fired. A single, sharp shot, straight to the chest. The guy fell to the ground with a thud, his limp body hitting the cold ground.

The problem wasn't that man. The problem was that I wasn't alone. I barely had time to react before another one stepped out of the shadows, lunging at me. We rolled on the ground, struggling. I felt his hands around my neck, squeezing with brutal force. My vision began to darken, but with one last effort, I swung my elbow back and punched him in the jaw with all my might. The guy let go of me long enough for me to draw my knife, and I sank the blade into his side.

I stood up quickly, panting, my hands bloody.

I continued down the aisles of the warehouse, passing stacks of dust-covered boxes. The

echoes of my footsteps resonated in the empty space. Every corner reminded me that I was in enemy territory, but I couldn't stop. If I stopped, Billy wouldn't get out of here alive. The Crow had made it clear that this was his hunt, but I wasn't about to become his prey.

Finally, I came to a door that seemed sealed, and I could hear the faint murmur of voices on the other side. I knew Billy was there. I prepared myself for the worst and, without hesitation, pulled the bolt. The door swung open with a bang.

Inside, Billy was tied to a chair, beaten but alive. My heart skipped a beat at the sight of him in that state. I had arrived in time.

I quickly approached him and began cutting the ropes holding him prisoner. "Owen? Finally!" Billy murmured in a hoarse voice, his face a mixture of relief and pain.

But just as I was about to release him, a figure stepped out of the shadows. Another outlaw, but this one was different. Calmer, more calculating. He had a scar on his cheek and a gun in his hand that was pointed directly at my chest.

"Don't move," he said in an icy voice, "or Billy will die."

It was an ultimatum. My eyes locked with his as I assessed the situation. I couldn't shoot without putting Billy at risk. I was trapped.

The man looked at me with a wicked smile,

enjoying the power he held at that moment. "You know that, don't you? The Raven is alive." His words were pure venom. "He's more alive than ever. And now... you're part of his plans, Stone. What you saw in the graveyard was just a small part of what's to come."

Without giving me time to react, the mercenary lunged at me. I blocked his attack with my arm and pushed him against the wall, hitting him with all my strength. The fight was short but brutal. Finally, I managed to grab him by the neck and, after a few seconds of struggle, I immobilized him.

As I held him against the wall, his face twisted in pain, but he chuckled at me anyway.

—It's too late, Stone. This is all part of a bigger plan. The Raven has you marked, and you don't even know it.

With one last push, I managed to knock the man unconscious to the ground. There was no more time to waste. I returned to Billy and finally freed him completely.

—Come on, buddy. We have to get out of here.

We left the warehouse as fast as our legs would carry us. The sky was already tinted red, announcing dawn, but the feeling of danger had not yet faded. I knew this was just beginning.

As we walked away from the warehouse, my gaze fell on a sheet of paper that had fallen from

the mercenary's pocket. I picked it up cautiously. Inside was a list. A list with names, all crossed out, except one: mine.

I felt a chill run down my spine. I had been targeted. The Crow didn't just want to toy with me, he wanted to finish me off. The message was clear. If I kept chasing him, it wouldn't be Billy who would pay the price. It would be me.

Hidden clues

The air in Gold Valley was thick with tension. Everyone was talking in whispers about "The Crow" and his crimes.

After leaving the warehouse, we continue our investigation to find The Crow.

We spent several days talking to every soul willing to share something useful. It took time, but we finally managed to put the pieces together: "El Cuervo" was behind several robberies and murders in the region, his signature was clear. They were not random acts and each one had a specific purpose.

—What do you think he wants, Owen? — Billy asked me, his eyes fixed on the road.

"Surely something more than gold or silver," I answered, feeling the weight of the words. "This is bigger. No one risks so much for a simple loot, and especially to appear from the dead."

Our search led us to an abandoned mansion in the hills west of Gold Valley. A place rumored to have belonged to a mining magnate who disappeared years ago. The townspeople believed it was cursed. To me, that was the sign that we were probably going to find something important.

We stopped in front of the dilapidated entrance. The mansion, with its cracked facade and broken windows, seemed to defy time. The wind blew through the branches of the trees,

creating a lament that echoed through the shadows.

"Are you sure this is the place?" Billy asked, adjusting his hat with shaking hands.

—I'm not sure, but it's the best we've got —I replied, patting him on the shoulder—. Let's move on, fear has never solved anything.

We entered in silence. The darkness inside was stifling, as if the mansion itself resisted the light from penetrating it. We walked cautiously, each step making the old wooden floor creak. At the end of the main hall, I saw something that caught my eye: a toppled bookshelf, with marks on the floor.

"Look at this," I whispered to Billy, pointing at the drag marks. "Someone moved this bookshelf recently."

With some effort we moved the bookcase, revealing a trapdoor in the floor. I slowly opened it, revealing a staircase leading down to a dark basement. I grabbed an oil lantern, lit it, and began to descend.

The basement was large, filled with dusty boxes and furniture covered with old sheets. The place looked abandoned, but there was something in the air that made me suspect we were not alone. In one corner, on a table, were scattered papers and maps of the region. One of them caught my attention immediately: a detailed map of Gold Valley with several red crosses.

"These are the robbery locations," I said, pointing to the map.

Billy, next to me, frowned, concentrating on the details.

—And here, he said, pointing to a particular cross, this is the Gold Valley bank. Do you think they're planning to rob it?

"I don't know," I admitted, studying the map. "But it seems that 'The Crow' won't settle for less."

Just as I turned to Billy to discuss our next move, I heard a noise above. The crunch of boots on the wooden floor. I pulled out my revolver and turned off the flashlight, motioning for Billy to crouch behind a stack of boxes. The footsteps multiplied, until they became a thud of boots echoing off the ceiling.

"There must be six or seven of them," I whispered. "They'll see the trapdoor open."

We stood still, listening. The noise stopped and I looked at Billy and saw the fear in his eyes. We were trapped.

A few seconds passed, and then I heard them descending. The stairs creaked under the weight of their bodies. The first to appear was a burly man, with a red handkerchief covering his face. Four others followed, each armed to the teeth. Finally, "The Crow" appeared, his imposing figure covering everything. His eyes, cold and calculating, scanned the basement.

"Search," he ordered, in a calm but firm voice.

One of his men came dangerously close to our position. I knew that within seconds we would be discovered. My mind was racing, searching for a way out. I looked around and saw an old window at the back, barely visible in the darkness. It looked just big enough for us to get through.

I signaled Billy and in one swift movement, I launched myself at the nearest man, knocking him down with one blow. A shot rang out and echoed through the basement, making noise off the walls.

—There they are! —one of the henchmen shouted, pointing his gun at us.

I didn't wait. I grabbed Billy by the arm and pushed him toward the window. Without thinking, he broke the glass with his elbow and slid through the gap. Meanwhile, gunfire whizzed around us. I felt the sting of a bullet grazing my shoulder, but I didn't stop. With one last push, I launched myself after Billy.

We fell outside, rolling on the wet grass. There was no time to stop. I heard the screams and curses of the men as they left the house.

—Come on, Billy! —I shouted, jumping up.

We stood up and ran to our horses, tied to some trees a few meters away. The sound of gunfire and the footsteps of men followed us closely. We mounted in one leap, and with a loud

"Gee!" we began to gallop at full speed.

The wind whipped my face as the landscape blurred around us. I could hear the thunder of enemy horses' hooves behind us. They weren't going to give up easily. But the terrain, filled with rocks and trees, was in our favor. I knew that if I could keep up the pace, we would leave them behind.

— Faster, Billy! —I shouted, seeing that his horse was beginning to fall behind.

Billy, pale and fear-eyed, tightened his reins and forced the animal to run faster. I did the same, feeling my horse respond strongly. I didn't look back. I didn't have to to know they were on our heels.

Suddenly, the sound of a gunshot echoed through the night. My horse whinnied, stumbling, and for a moment I thought it was all over. But the animal recovered and we continued forward. I felt the warm blood running down my wounded shoulder, but I ignored the pain. We had to keep going.

Finally, after what seemed like an eternity, the sounds of the pursuers began to fade away. When the sound of hooves and the voices of the men of "El Cuervo" became a distant echo, I knew that we were not being followed.

We stopped by a stream and I stumbled off my horse. Billy slid to the ground too, panting. We were both covered in dust and sweat, our

hearts pounding like hammers.

"That... was... intense," he managed to say between breaths.

"Yes, it was," I replied, letting out a sigh of relief. "But we did it."

We sat by the stream, letting the sound of the water calm us. I knew that "The Raven" would not give up so easily. We had taken something more valuable than his map: the certainty that his plans were not as impenetrable as he believed. And that, in this fight, was a powerful weapon.

Lost testimony

Once we managed to get out of the clutches of "The Crow" and his gang, my mind didn't stop working. I knew we had found something important in that mansion. Although the documents we took were full of confusing notes and maps of the region, there was one name that stood out among all that chaos: Jasper O'Neill.

Jasper was an old acquaintance of the underworld. A snitch who always had an eye on the movements of the outlaws in the region. If anyone knew anything about "The Crow" and his plans, it would be him. So, after recovering by the stream, we decided to look for him.

It wasn't hard to find him. Jasper had his hideout just outside Gold Valley, a small cabin hidden among the pines. The moon was high in the sky when we arrived, casting long shadows across the road. Billy and I approached cautiously, knowing Jasper was as dangerous as the information he sold.

"Let me handle this," I said to Billy before knocking on the door. I didn't want the kid to get nervous and make a mistake.

—Who is it? —a hoarse voice answered from inside.

"Owen Stone," I replied. "I need to talk to you."

We heard a heavy footsteps and then the door opened just a few inches. A pair of small,

suspicious eyes stared at me before the door swung open.

—Owen! —Jasper said with a toothless grin. —It's been a while since you've been around here. What brings you to this corner of the world?

"I need information about The Crow," I said bluntly. "We know he's planning something big, and you're going to tell us about it."

Jasper's smile faded a little, but he still maintained his jovial tone.

—Oh, "The Crow", huh? That black bird is trouble, that's for sure and it seems to have been resurrected or did it never die? Who knows. But... information comes at a price, you know.

"You're lucky I'm not charging you," I replied with a cold smile. "Talk, Jasper. What do you know?"

Jasper was silent for a moment, assessing the situation. Finally, he nodded and invited us in. The cabin was dim, with only an oil lamp illuminating the main room. We sat around a rickety table, and Jasper began to talk.

—I've heard rumors that The Crow is recruiting men for a big hit. Something at the Gold Valley bank, he said, leaning on the table. He's been gathering dynamite, and it's not for opening a bottle of whiskey.

Billy and I exchanged glances. It was just what we feared.

—When are you going to do it? —I asked.

"I don't know that," Jasper said, shrugging. "But there's more. They say he has someone inside the bank, a traitor who feeds him information from within."

This made things complicated. Not only did we have to worry about "El Cuervo" and his gang, but also about someone who was making his job easier from within. Time was running out.

—Who is it? —I asked, feeling the tension rising. —Who's helping him?

Before Jasper could respond, the window behind him shattered into a thousand pieces. The sound of a gunshot echoed through the cabin, and Jasper fell back, clutching his chest. A gasp escaped his mouth before he collapsed to the ground, motionless.

—No! —Billy screamed, recoiling in horror.

I pulled out my revolver and turned to the window, looking for the shooter. Outside, I saw a dark figure slipping quickly through the trees.

—Stay here! —I ordered Billy, and I rushed toward the door.

I ran out, my heart pounding in my ears. I could still see the killer as a dark flash in the gloom. I fired a couple of shots, but he was moving fast, zigzagging through the trees.

—Stop! —I screamed, even though I knew it was useless.

The killer reached the end of the forest and, in

one swift movement, jumped through a window of an old building. I stopped right in front of the structure, breathing heavily. I knew that going in alone was crazy, but I couldn't let him get away.

—I'm going to get him! —I shouted towards the cabin, hoping Billy would hear.

I entered carefully, keeping my gun ready. My eyes slowly adjusted to the darkness as I made my way through the abandoned interior of the building. Everything was silent, save for the sound of my own footsteps on the dusty floor.

Suddenly, I saw him. The killer was just a few feet away, at the opposite end of the room, preparing to escape through another window. Without thinking, I aimed and fired. The bullet hit the wall next to his head, and he stopped dead in his tracks, turning to look at me.

—Don't move! —I warned him, my voice echoing in the enclosed space.

The man looked at me with a mocking smile. I could see the glint in his eyes from a distance, and I knew he had no intention of giving up.

"Too late, Stone," he said, and with a quick movement, he launched himself towards the window.

I fired again, but he was already out. I ran to the window and watched him disappear into the darkness, his figure melting into the night. I cursed under my breath and lowered the gun. He had gotten away from me.

I went back to the cabin, where Billy was standing over Jasper's body, his eyes filled with tears and his hands shaking.

"He's dead, Owen," she said, her voice breaking. "Just when we were going to get the answers."

I walked over and knelt beside the body, feeling the frustration and anger burning inside me. Jasper had been a criminal, a snitch, and a traitor, but at that moment he was the only lead we had.

"I know, Billy," I said, putting a hand on his shoulder. "But this isn't over. We'll find The Crow, no matter what it takes."

As I looked at Jasper's lifeless body, I knew this was about more than just stopping a criminal. This was a war, and "The Crow" had just thrown the first punch. But if he thought he could intimidate us, he was sorely mistaken.

I stood up, staring into the darkness beyond the broken window. The killer might have gotten away this time, but he wasn't going to run forever.

—Come on, Billy. We've got a lot of work ahead of us.

Billy nodded, wiping his eyes with his sleeve. The sadness in his eyes turned to determination. He knew he had crossed a line from which there was no turning back.

—We will find him, Owen. And he will pay

for this.

"Yes, Billy," I said, clenching my fist tightly. "I can assure you of that."

Ambush in the desert

Dawn caught up with us riding into the desert, following the trail of Jasper's killer, whose name remained a mystery. We had followed his tracks all night, driven by the urgency to catch the only man who could give us answers about "The Raven." We knew this could be a trap, but we had no other choice.

The landscape was barren and desolate. Red sands stretched as far as the eye could see, broken by sharp rock formations that rose like the teeth of a sleeping monster. Beside me, Billy rode silently, his young face marked by fatigue and determination. We hadn't spoken much since we left Jasper's cabin, each lost in our own thoughts.

—Do you think they're waiting for us? —he finally asked, breaking the silence.

"You always have to expect an ambush, Billy," I replied, adjusting my hat to protect myself from the sun that was beginning to peek through. The heat was beginning to make itself felt, and it was only the first hours of the day. "It's the only way you won't get caught off guard."

We rode for several hours, following the killer's trail through the desert. He was a good tracker, good enough to keep me from getting lost. His tracks wound through the dunes and headed toward a narrow canyon, an ideal place to set a trap. The high, rocky walls formed a natural

maze, blocking out the sunlight and casting dark shadows on the sandy ground.

"I don't like this, Owen," Billy said, his voice barely above a whisper. "It's like we're being led to something."

"I know," I replied, stopping to survey the terrain. "But we don't have much choice. If that man leads us to The Crow, we have to keep going."

We dismounted and continued on foot, leading the animals by the reins to prevent the echo of their hooves from alerting anyone hiding among the rocks. Each step echoed like thunder in the deathly silence of the canyon. In the distance, I saw a small camp: a few tents and armed men around a campfire. I crouched behind a rock formation, and Billy stood beside me, his head barely peeking out.

"Look," I said quietly, pointing toward the camp. "There it is."

The man who had killed Jasper was talking to another man, pointing in our direction. I felt a chill run down my spine. There was something about his posture, the way he moved, that I didn't like. Like he was expecting us to do exactly what we were doing.

—Do you think he knows we're here? —Billy whispered, his hand shaking slightly on the grip of his revolver.

"He knows," I replied, trying to remain calm.

"And he probably has more men waiting."

We stood still, watching. There were at least six men in the camp, and surely more hiding among the rocks. We couldn't face them head on, but retreating now would mean losing the trail. Damn. We were between a rock and a hard place.

"Let's get a little closer," I told Billy, even though I knew it was risky. We needed a better view of the terrain before we made any moves.

We crept forward, hugging the canyon walls, moving slowly. Every sound, every crunch of sand beneath our feet, seemed to echo like a gunshot. When we were close enough to hear their conversation, I leaned forward, straining my ears.

"…they'll come straight here," Jasper's killer said in a calm, confident voice. "When they do, we'll be ready."

—Are you sure they will come? —the other man asked, in a skeptical tone.

—Of course. Stone won't let the opportunity pass him by. He thinks he has the upper hand, but he's really just a mouse running into a trap.

Billy looked at me with wide eyes, and I nodded. We were exactly where they wanted us to be. Before I could decide our next move, Jasper's killer turned and looked directly at where we were hiding.

—They're here! —he shouted, drawing his

weapon.

There was no time to think. I grabbed Billy by the arm and dragged him backwards, running towards the mouth of the canyon. The roar of gunfire filled the air, bullets whistling around us. We took cover behind a large rock, gasping, as the echo of the shots reverberated off the walls.

—They've got us trapped! —Billy shouted, trying to load his revolver with shaking hands.

"I know, but we have to stay calm," I said, leaning out to assess the situation. Two men had positioned themselves at the top of the canyon, blocking our exit, and four others were advancing toward us with their weapons drawn.

— Any ideas? —Billy asked, his voice thick with desperation.

"Yes, not to let us be killed," I replied, trying to keep my tone light despite the danger. I knew we were in a critical position. Trying to fight was suicidal, but surrendering meant giving our lives to "The Crow."

—Stone! —the assassin's voice echoed through the canyon, loud and clear. —Surrender now, and "The Crow" may let you live!

I didn't respond immediately. I knew his words were poison, designed to break us before they could kill us. But if there was any chance of survival, we had to play this hand carefully.

—You have nowhere to go, Stone. This time, there is no escape.

I looked at Billy. His face was pale, but I saw the spark of determination in his eyes. He was brave, I didn't doubt that, but I didn't want to see him die here, in this damn desert.

—Okay! —I shouted back. —We surrender.

I saw the men slowly advance with their guns pointed at us. Jasper's killer was smiling with his gun drawn, ready to shoot at any suspicious movement.

"I knew you were smart, Stone," he said, coming closer. "The Crow wants to talk to you. And believe me, it's best to do so without confrontation."

I stared back at him, trying to calculate my options. Then, I heard a distant noise, like a dull roar echoing across the desert. The men around me turned, confused, and I saw my chance.

But before I could act, I felt a sharp blow to my head. Everything went black instantly, and the last thing I heard was the laughter of Jasper's killer, echoing in the darkness that enveloped me.

A special crack

Consciousness returned to me like a soft whisper amidst the chaos. I was lying on the ground, the taste of dirt and blood mixing in my mouth. When I finally opened my eyes, all I saw was darkness and desert dust dancing in the shafts of light filtering through the rocks. It took me a moment to realize that Billy was beside me, helping me up.

—Owen, are you okay? —she asked, her voice full of concern.

—Yes... I think so —I answered, massaging my head where the blow had been the hardest. —What happened?

— We escaped! —he said excitedly, hiding the tension in his voice. —It was a total mess, but we managed to escape.

I looked around. The darkness of the canyon had provided us with the necessary cover. I remembered the critical moment when Jasper's killer's men had surrounded us. It had been a game of nerves, sweat dripping down my brow as we waited for the perfect moment to escape. The distraction of the distant roar had been our salvation, and it had been in that instant of chaos, as everyone turned to look at the horizon, that we had darted toward a crack in the rock that had led us to a detour in the canyon. That small opening had allowed us to evade our captors, and now we wanted to get back to the village, our

hearts beating a mile a minute.

We mounted our horses again, eager to get away from this deadly trap. The walk back to the village seemed longer than I remembered. The hot sand stuck to our boots, and the air was thick with a mixture of dust and the smell of sweat. When we finally arrived, the familiarity of the place brought me some relief, but also a sense of unease.

We headed to our office and I went straight to my desk, where a dark shadow loomed over a crumpled piece of paper. There was no mistaking it for a note that had been left recently. I took it in my hands, my heart racing as I read the words written in firm handwriting: "I've been watching you. You must stop before it's too late."

"What does it say?" Billy asked, moving closer, anxiety palpable in his voice.

"Someone is warning me," I said, frowning as I read over and over again. The feeling of being watched intensified. It was as if a ghost from the past had come back to haunt me.

The silence in the office became heavy, almost oppressive. I looked out the window at the main street, where the shadows were beginning to lengthen with the twilight. I remembered that during the afternoon, the town had been bustling, but now an eerie calm had settled over it.

"Who could have left this note?" Billy asked,

breaking the silence. His gaze reflected both concern and curiosity.

"It could be someone close to me," I replied, feeling the weight of paranoia begin to crush me. "It's like the Crow isn't just after me, but there's someone else, someone who knows my steps, my weaknesses."

"That's disturbing," Billy nodded, his voice sounding like a whisper. "Maybe someone who's been watching everything from the shadows."

The atmosphere became more tense. The idea of a traitor among us began to take shape. Every ally, every acquaintance that crossed my mind became a potential enemy. In this world of mistrust, even the smallest gesture could hide dark intentions.

"We have to find out," Billy said, his voice determined. "We can't let this turn into a shadow game. We need to identify who we have to fear."

"You're right," I replied, setting the note down on the desk, urgency beginning to creep into every word. "But first, we need to rest. We've been on the brink of death today, and we need to regain our strength before we continue."

As I sat back in my chair, a wave of exhaustion washed over me. But I couldn't stop thinking about the warning written in that letter. Who wanted to play with us? And what did they really want?

As the afternoon turned into evening, the

sunlight faded, leaving only a faint glow on the horizon. The atmosphere of the village became eerie, the murmurs of the people and the distant sound of music from a hall faded into the air. Everything seemed more somber, more laden with secrets.

It was then that I heard the door creak. I turned quickly, my instincts kicking in. There, in the doorway, stood a familiar face, but one I had thought lost in time. It was Clara, an old friend and ally from my bounty hunting days, whose presence had been a ray of light in dark times.

"Hi Owen…" she said, her voice shaking as her eyes fell on me, full of concern.

"Clara, what are you doing here?" I asked, feeling a whirlwind of emotions. Surprise filled me and the past began to flow back, bringing back memories of laughter, shared struggles and betrayals.

"I came to warn you. You are not safe," he said, and the seriousness of his voice extinguished any trace of joy in my chest.

My heart raced. Not only had we escaped the ambush; now it seemed we were facing an even greater threat. Clara had always been cunning, able to see what others couldn't. I moved closer, trying to decipher the urgency in her gaze.

—What do you mean? —I asked, trying to remain calm despite my growing anxiety.

"There's something bigger than the Crow at

play. I've been hearing rumors… and there are those who want to see you out of the picture, Owen. They're willing to do anything," he warned, his gaze locked on mine, searching for answers.

The mention of a greater threat chilled my blood. As I tried to process his words, I realized that Clara's return was not just a chance encounter. It was a warning, a call to action in the midst of the danger that loomed over us.

"We must act quickly," I said determinedly. "We cannot allow ourselves to be caught off guard."

Billy, who had been listening intently, nodded. "Clara, tell us. What do you know?"

As Clara began to recount the rumors she had heard, the feeling that a ghost from the past had returned to alter the course of our lives grew stronger. Words of warning rang in my ears, and the echo of those who had fallen into the darkness of this world began to reverberate.

What had started as a simple quest for justice was turning into a deadly game with forces he couldn't fully understand. With every word, the truth grew more complex, and at the heart of it all, a menacing shadow still lurked, ready to unleash chaos.

The deadly trap

The atmosphere in the office was tense and filled with uncertainty. Clara's warning still echoed in my mind like a haunting echo. After deliberating for a few minutes, I decided that we could not stand by and do nothing. We had to act and take down The Crow before we acted.

"Billy, we need to follow the lead Clara mentioned," I said, looking at my young companion, who was just as eager to do justice as I was. "She spoke of rumors about an abandoned mine east of here. They say El Cuervo and his gang have been using that place to hide out and plan their next moves."

— A mine? Sounds like a perfect ambush spot, Billy replied, his face reflecting the mix of determination and fear we both felt.

As we prepared, the air in the office was filled with the impending sense of danger. We armed ourselves with our pistols, making sure we had plenty of ammunition, and set off towards the mine with the afternoon sun beating down on our heads.

The path to the mine was a dusty trail, surrounded by cacti and rocks. With each step we took, the atmosphere became more oppressive, as if the earth itself was warning us of what awaited us. The mine was located in an isolated canyon, and as we approached, a feeling of unease began to take hold of me. The darkness

of the place seemed to swallow the light of day.

"Owen, are you sure this is a good idea?" Billy asked, his voice filled with a mix of anxiety and common sense.

"We have to find out the truth, Billy. If we find evidence of The Crow, we can catch him and put an end to this once and for all. We can't let fear paralyze us," I replied, although inside, a part of me also feared what I might find.

With oil lamp in hand, we entered the mine. The walls were covered in moisture, and the echo of our footsteps reverberated in the darkness. The air was heavy and cold, an eerie contrast to the heat outside. As we moved forward, the silence was almost palpable, interrupted only by the distant dripping of water.

The inside of the mine was a labyrinth of tunnels and passages, some only dimly lit by our lamp. The dancing light cast eerie shadows on the walls, and with every step we took, the tension grew. I remembered stories about these mines, of the men who had worked in them, and of the dangers that lurked in the darkness.

After a few minutes of searching, we found a larger space where footprints were evident. I could sense that we were close. As I examined the place, a trail of abandoned objects and debris indicated that there had been recent activity. Adrenaline began to flow through my veins.

"Look at this," Billy said, pointing to an old

sack sticking out of a pile of rocks. I opened it, and there I found documents confirming the activities of the "Crow." There were detailed plans for robberies and extortions, and everything pointed to an upcoming hit in the town.

"This is incredible, Billy. This could be the key to knowing where The Crow is going next," I said, feeling hope spark within me. But just as I was about to put the documents away, a thud echoed through the mine.

The sound was getting louder, like an ominous creaking that echoed through the walls. My heart stopped for a moment and then began to pound.

—Owen, what was that?! —Billy asked, his voice full of fear.

"I don't know," I replied, frowning. I knew something wasn't right. Without a second thought, I decided we should get out of there. But before we could make any move, the ground began to shake.

— We have to go! —I shouted, and we both started running towards the entrance, but the echo of the crunching intensified. The walls of the mine seemed to collapse on us. As we ran, large blocks of rock began to fall, and the sound of the collapse became a deafening chaos.

—Hurry, Owen! —Billy shouted, as we hurried toward the exit. The path we had taken was crumbling behind us, as if the mine was

determined to trap us.

Billy's warning screams echoed in my ears, and the dust began to blind us. Finally, we reached the exit, but just as we were about to cross the threshold, the roar reached its peak. A large wooden beam, held together by time and neglect, snapped and fell, blocking our only way out.

"No!" I screamed, lunging forward, but the dust was too thick, and the air was filled with the despair of what seemed to be an imminent end. The walls continued to shake, and the mine was collapsing around us.

Billy and I looked back, where the darkness swallowed the light from the entrance. With no way out, our chances of escape vanished before our eyes. Sweat dripped down my forehead, and the reality of our situation settled over me like a dark fog.

"Owen, there's no time!" Billy said, his voice shaking with terror as he searched for a way out.

—Keep looking! —I replied, feeling panic begin to invade my mind. The mine creaked and shook, and the sound of falling rocks echoed like a death chant.

At that critical moment, a spark of determination lit up my mind. I remember the stories of former miners who had found ways to escape from similar situations. I knew time was running out, but there was still hope. With a firm voice, I tried to calm Billy down.

—Billy, stay calm. If there's a way out, we'll find it. There must be tunnels that have remained intact. Come on!

As the chaos continued around us, we began to explore the walls of the mine, feeling around for a crack or a hidden path. My hands were full of dust, and the air grew heavier with every second. Billy began to tap his foot on the ground, searching for a different sound, something that would tell us there was more to this death trap.

— Owen, here! —he suddenly shouted, his voice echoing through the mine. I quickly approached his side, and he pointed to a small space between the stones.

With an effort, we began to move the rocks, removing the loose stones that obstructed the path. Each block we removed made the structure of the mine tremble, and the sound of the collapse continued to resonate like a drum in our hearts. The pressure increased, and the adrenaline pushed us to continue working.

Finally, we managed to make a hole big enough for us to squeeze through. Billy was the first to slip through, and with a last effort, I managed to follow him. We fell into a small side tunnel, and the echo of our passage became a whisper.

— Are you okay? —I asked as I stood up, brushing the dust off my clothes. Billy nodded, still visibly nervous, but there was a glimmer of

hope in his eyes.

"I think we're safe, at least for now," he replied, looking down the dark tunnel in front of us.

We started to move forward, using the oil lamp we found. As we walked, I felt a mixture of relief and anxiety. I knew we had escaped imminent death.

A while later, we found a small group of rocks where the light barely filtered through. As we got closer, we discovered more documents scattered on the ground, similar to the ones we had found before, but now with blood marks on them. My thoughts raced; the "Crow" must be closer than we thought.

As we looked through the papers, we realized they contained more plans, more robberies, and a name: a possible informant. Time seemed to stand still as I read aloud. Just as I was about to put the documents away, a thud echoed behind us.

The ground began to shake again, and a warning cry burst from my lips. The mine was more alive than ever.

"Let's run!" I shouted, and we both began to move quickly through the tunnel. The walls seemed to close in around us, and the air grew heavy with the threat of another collapse.

At the end of the tunnel, we found a wooden staircase that seemed to lead to the surface.

There was no time to think. We began to climb, step by step, while the echo of the collapse resonated behind us. When we reached the top, we found ourselves in front of a rusty iron door.

"Push it!" I shouted to Billy, and together we threw ourselves at the door, which opened with a painful creak. The sunlight hit us hard, as if welcoming us into the outside world.

"We did it!" Billy exclaimed, his face illuminated by the light. But before we could breathe a sigh of relief, we heard the sound of hurried footsteps and voices in the distance. The hunt wasn't over.

"Let's not waste time," I said, and we both ran to the safety of the nearby bushes. We hid, listening to the voices of El Cuervo's men approaching the mine, wondering what had happened.

With my heart pounding, I knew that the death trap we had faced was just part of the game.

One step forward

After losing our pursuers, we stopped to rest.

"We need to get back to the office and review those mine documents," I told Billy, my voice firm despite my exhaustion.

Billy nodded, and we both headed back to town, walking in silence as our minds continued to replay what we had just experienced. The echoes of the mine still rang in my head, but I knew we couldn't waste any time. The Crow was always one step ahead, and we had to change that.

When we arrived at the office, the familiarity of the place gave me a momentary sense of security. I closed the door behind us and laid the papers on the table. The oil lamp cast long shadows on the walls as we meticulously reviewed each page.

"Look at this," Billy said suddenly, pointing at one of the documents. I walked over and saw what he had found.

Among the detailed plans for robbery and extortion, a name appeared that we had not seen before: Jansen. I looked at him carefully, trying to remember if I had heard him before.

"He works at the bank," I murmured, immediately remembering his face. He was one of the town's tellers. Discreet, quiet, and never called attention to himself. The kind of person who could easily go unnoticed and who had

access to sensitive information.

—Do you think he'll be Crow's confidant? — Billy asked, sounding incredulous.

"I don't know," I replied with determination. Now, everything made sense.

Wasting no time, we prepared to go after him. This time, the advantage could be ours. For the first time, we had the chance to get ahead of the Crow and stop his plans before he could act.

We left the office and walked quickly through the streets of the village. The shadows of the night were beginning to lengthen, and the atmosphere was filled with an eerie silence. By now, Jansen would be closing the bank.

When we arrived at his small house, there was no light in the windows, but I knew he was there. We approached cautiously, keeping the sound of our footsteps to a minimum. Billy stayed near the back door while I moved to the window. I peered through the glass and saw him inside, moving through papers and counting money. He was nervous.

"He's inside. Let's go in carefully," I said quietly to Billy.

We quietly opened the door, and within seconds, we were inside. Jansen didn't even have time to react when I grabbed him by the shirt and pushed him against the wall.

— Jansen! —I roared, my face just inches from his. —We know what you're doing. You

work for the Crow. When's the bank heist going to happen?

His face filled with panic, and he began to babble something incoherent. He was not a man accustomed to confrontation, and the pressure was breaking him.

—I... I don't know what you're talking about, Owen —she said, her voice shaking.

I pushed him harder against the wall, my patience running out.

—Don't play with me, Jansen. We know you've been passing information to him. If you don't talk, you're not leaving this house.

Billy, who was standing at the door, was looking at me with a mixture of concern and expectation, waiting to see if Jansen would break.

—All right, all right! —he finally cried, throwing up his hands in surrender. —They... they're coming tomorrow morning. They're going to rob the bank right after it opens. That's all I know!

My heart raced as I heard his words. For the first time, we had the chance to get ahead.

"Thank you for your cooperation," I said, letting go of him.

We dropped Jansen off at his house, making sure he couldn't warn anyone. On the way out, I signaled to Billy to head back to the office and plan our next move.

"Now we know when and where, Billy.

Tomorrow, we'll put an end to this," I said, my voice filled with the determination that burned inside me.

—Yes, but we have to be careful, Owen. The Raven isn't going down easily, Billy replied, his tone filled with concern but also determination.

I nodded. The Raven was clever, but this time we would be waiting for him.

Silent Ambush

The next morning came with an air of tension that could be cut with a knife. The sun was barely rising over the hills when Billy and I arrived at the bank, ready for the showdown. The bank manager, nervous and sweaty-handed, was waiting for us in his office, his look reflecting the anxiety of someone who was not used to this kind of situation.

—Are you sure today is the day? —he asked, clutching his handkerchief in his hands.

"Everything points to yes," I replied, trying to remain calm, although inside, something didn't fit.

We had agreed to do what seemed the most prudent thing to do. Billy and I would disguise ourselves as cashiers, while the sheriff, along with some of his men, mingled among the "customers." Everyone was armed and ready for the arrival of The Crow and his gang. We had the upper hand for once, and now all that was left to do was wait.

The bank routine began like any other day. Some citizens began arriving early to make their deposits, unaware of the ambush that was underway. From my position behind the counter, I watched every movement, every shadow that passed in front of the windows.

The sheriff, hidden among the customers, looked calm, but he knew that look; he too was

on alert, waiting for the signal. Each of his men kept their hands close to their guns, camouflaged among the people coming and going, going about their daily business.

Time passed and the bank continued with its normal activity. The minutes ticked by, and with them, the suspicion. We had waited all morning, but there was no sign of the Cuervo gang.

Would he have found out about the trap?

The clock on the wall read twelve o'clock. Too much time had passed without any sign of them. I approached Billy, who was trying to appear calm while he concealed himself by placing some documents.

"Something's not right," I whispered. "They should have shown up hours ago."

Billy nodded silently, but said nothing. I could see in his eyes the same doubt I felt inside myself. The Raven was cunning, but we had been careful this time. How could they have known?

I crept up to the sheriff, who was sitting in one of the chairs near the door, his gaze fixed on the entrance.

"They're not coming," I murmured. "What could have happened?"

The sheriff frowned, his fingers drumming uneasily on the arm of his chair.

"They may have changed their plans," he whispered, not taking his eyes off the door. "Or someone warned them."

That last sentence echoed in my head. If the Crow had been warned, who would have done it? I immediately thought of Jansen, the bank employee who had given us the information. Could he have betrayed us, playing both sides?

"I'm going to find Jansen," I said quietly. "He could be the key."

The sheriff nodded, not taking his eyes off the entrance. He knew time was running out.

I left the bank with Billy and we quickly headed to Jansen's house. When we arrived, I knocked hard on the door, but there was no answer. I tried several times, but only the echo of my knocks reverberated inside the house.

"Something's not right," Billy muttered. "Did he give us away?"

I pushed the door open, which opened easily. When I entered, everything was quiet, and a feeling of emptiness hung in the air. We searched the entire house, but Jansen was not there. He had left the table in a mess, as if he had left in a hurry.

"Damn, I knew we couldn't trust him," I growled, clenching my fists.

Billy, sifting through a pile of papers on his desk, found something: a clumsily written note, as if he had left it in a hurry.

"They know. Be careful."

The Crow knew about the bank scam. And if Jansen was involved, it meant he had been

playing both sides. He knew too much, and now it was clear they were looking for him, or worse, they already had him.

"We can't waste any more time," I said with determination. "If the Crow didn't attack the bank, he must be planning something bigger."

—What do we do? —Billy asked as we walked out of the house, the tension between us growing.

—Let's go back to the bank. We need to talk to the sheriff and change our focus. Then... we find Jansen.

Confrontation

Back at the bench, Janse was in his place, as if nothing had happened.

— What does this note mean, Janse? —I shouted, grabbing him by the neck in fury.

"It's not what it looks like, Mr. Owen," Janse stammered, his eyes wide with wonder. "It's a trick. The Crow was planning to rob this bank or that one, and I told him the other one was under surveillance."

Reluctantly, we let him go. We decided to wait, giving him the benefit of the doubt, to see if his words were true.

"Here they come," Billy muttered, his hand shaking slightly on the butt of his hidden pistol.

"Stay calm," I said, though I could feel the cold sweat on my back. The horses' hooves came closer and closer, until at last we saw their dark figures moving like shadows through the morning mist.

Through the bank windows, we watched as the Crow and his gang dismounted with agile, disciplined movements. Their figures were unmistakable: five men with scarves covering half their faces, wide-brimmed hats, and gleaming weapons sticking out from their belts. The Crow, the undisputed leader, had a presence that made the air in the room feel heavier. Tall, erect, with a scar running down his cheek, he advanced with a confidence that only someone

who has mastered fear could display.

"They're here," I whispered to the sheriff, who nodded almost imperceptibly from his place by the window.

The Crow pushed open the doors of the bank calmly, as if he were entering a business meeting and not a robbery. His footsteps echoed on the wooden floor of the bank, making each second seem longer. The other four men in his gang entered behind him, spreading out across the room. One stayed near the door, watching the street. The others moved easily among the "customers," as if assessing each possible threat.

"Good morning, gentlemen," said the Raven, with an almost mocking smile in his deep voice, as he paused in front of the counter. "We've come for some money, if you don't mind."

It was a simple statement, but the underlying threat was palpable. We were dealing with a man accustomed to getting his way, someone who calculated every move with precision.

—Sure... What kind of transaction do you want to make? —I answered with my eyes downcast and my voice as firm as I could, pretending to be a bank employee as we had planned.

"A very big one," the Raven replied, coming a little closer. His eyes locked on mine, searching for any sign, any clue that something was wrong.

I noticed that one of his men, a burly guy with

a scar on his neck, had started walking among the "customers." His eyes scanned every corner of the bank, and I could see him frown as he stopped next to one of the sheriff's men, who was trying to remain unnoticed.

The Raven noticed it too. I saw it in his eyes: a flash of suspicion, as if a small piece of the puzzle had fallen into place. Slowly, he tilted his head, looking around more intently. His smile disappeared.

—Wait a minute... —he murmured, his tone now more serious. Suddenly, his eyes returned to me, as if they had found something that confirmed their suspicions. —What's going on here?

I felt the air growing thicker, danger imminent. Billy, next to me, started to reach for his gun, but I stopped him with a slight gesture. Not yet. If the Crow noticed the ambush too soon, everything could fall apart.

One of the Raven's men made a subtle signal from the doorway. There was something in his body language that conveyed alarm. The Raven needed no more. His gaze hardened, and his voice turned harsh.

— It's a trap! —he shouted, drawing his revolver with terrifying speed.

At that instant, chaos erupted. The Crow stepped back as his men drew their weapons. The burly man among the customers threw a

table aside, using it as a makeshift shield. The other three began firing toward the windows, covering their retreat. The bank's glass shattered, and the echoes of gunfire echoed throughout the street.

— Don't let them get away! —the sheriff shouted, drawing his own revolver and firing toward the door.

We ran for the entrance, but the Crow and his gang had already leapt onto their horses with disconcerting agility. Shots flew around them, but they managed to get away with a timing that only years of experience could provide. In the blink of an eye, they were already mounted, speeding away.

—Damn it! —I cursed, chasing after them as the bullets continued to fly.

The Raven, leading his group, turned on his horse and fired a couple more times before disappearing at the end of the street. For a moment, the sound of hooves and the whistling of the wind were the only sounds. Then silence fell over the place again.

We had been so close... But somehow, the Raven had sensed the trap before we could catch him.

Unexpected return

The bank fell silent after the failed attempt. The air felt heavy, as if the frustration of having let the Crow escape hung in every corner. The sheriff and his men were scattered, some checking the broken windows, others picking up spent bullets. All indications were that the plan, though sound, had failed. Billy and I exchanged tired glances as we made our way back into the bank.

—We had the chance, but... —Billy whispered to me, his voice dragged with frustration.

"This isn't the time for regrets," I interrupted, trying to stay focused. I knew all was not lost yet. We could still find another way to catch him. We walked over to the counter, our hearts beating slower now that the tension had eased.

As we packed away our weapons and organized the papers we had left behind before the confrontation, the silence in the street began to feel too deep. Too... empty. It was a stillness that didn't fit the chaos we had experienced moments before. Something didn't fit.

Suddenly, a distant noise broke the stillness. The sound of horse hooves, fast and increasing, began to echo in the distance. At first, we didn't pay much attention, thinking it might be the usual cowboys or farmers going about their daily chores. But as they came closer, the sound began to sink into our bones. Something about the way

the hooves hit the ground struck us as strange, threatening.

—Do you hear that? —Billy looked at me with his eyes half closed and his hand already resting on his revolver.

I headed for the broken window, the same one through which the Crow and his gang had escaped minutes before. As I looked out, my heart skipped a beat.

— It's him! —I shouted, unable to hide the surprise in my voice.

In the distance, through the dust raised by the hooves, I saw the unmistakable figures of the Crow and his band, riding back towards the bank. This time, they were coming in closer formation, with a speed and determination we had not seen before. The Crow was in front, and although the distance was still considerable, his black hat and the scar on his face were visible as a constant threat.

"It can't be..." Billy muttered in disbelief, approaching the window.

The sheriff, who was organizing his men inside the bank, heard our commotion and rushed toward us.

"What's going on?" he asked, but when he looked out at the street, his face paled. "Damn it, they're coming back!"

"Why?" I asked, as we watched the Raven and his band approach at speed. Something didn't

add up. They had fled, and yet here they were, riding back toward the trap they had already discovered.

The sheriff cursed under his breath, signaling his men to get back into position. But the bewilderment was still there in each of us. What had changed? Why were they coming back?

"Maybe they want more than just money," Billy muttered, his gaze fixed on the Raven.

"Or maybe it's a distraction," I replied, thinking of the cryptic note we'd found earlier. Maybe there was something else at play, something we hadn't considered.

We quickly returned to our positions. The sheriff's men gathered behind the counters and walls, ready for anything. Everything was silent, except for the sound of hooves getting closer and closer.

"Get ready!" the sheriff shouted, as the men adjusted their revolvers and took better cover.

The riders arrived in front of the bank in a frenzy of dust and noise. The Raven, in front, stopped his horse dead, his eyes scanning the building like a hawk looking for its prey. For a moment, it seemed as if all time had stopped. The Raven stared at us with an intensity that pierced the walls of the bank.

But instead of charging forward, the Raven gave a hand signal, and his band scattered, surrounding the bank.

"This doesn't look good," I said, lowering my voice.

The sheriff gritted his teeth, watching as the Raven's men moved around the building.

"They're going to surround us," he muttered.

The Crow calmly dismounted, his boots echoing on the dusty ground as he approached the bank entrance, his hand resting on the grip of his revolver. He didn't say a word, but his presence spoke for itself. Slowly, he pushed open the doors of the bank, and entered with the same calm he had had on the first robbery attempt.

—What do you think you're doing? —the sheriff growled, rising from his hiding place with his revolver pointed directly at Raven.

The Raven replied with a cold, almost mocking smile.

"I just came to finish what I started," he replied, his voice low and soft, but with a palpable menace. "This time… there will be no cheating."

The roar of bullets

Time seemed to stop the moment his men, until then motionless around the bench, began to move like shadows.

The roar filled the air. The bank windows turned into a shower of glass, as bullets flew across the room. The sheriff and his men, hidden behind counters and walls, began to return fire, each shot echoing off the wooden walls. The tension had stagnated into a scene of pure chaos.

—Take cover! —the sheriff shouted as bullets whistled through the air.

The Crow, standing near the door, darted to the side, dodging the bullets with quick, precise movements. At his signal, the gang began to shoot mercilessly, taking up strategic positions along the street. The Crow's men were no gang of outlaws. They knew what they were doing, and each shot was calculated to keep us at bay, pinned behind the counter.

Billy, his face covered in dust, was shooting towards the entrance, barely keeping his head out to avoid being hit by the bullets. The noise was deafening, each explosion resonated in our ears like thunder, making the walls of the bank tremble.

Suddenly, from the dust rising in the street, something we had not expected appeared: a cart pulled by two horses was rapidly approaching the bank. At first glance, it looked like just an

ordinary transport cart, covered by a tarp. But when one of the Raven's men jumped off his horse and pushed off the tarp, something much more lethal was revealed.

—Damn, they have a fucking machine gun! — I exclaimed in horror.

The machine gun, a rusty but fully functional Gatling gun, came into view. The Raven man cranked the handle, and the roar of the machine filled the air. A torrent of bullets began to pour out of the weapon, piercing the wooden walls of the bank as if they were paper. We barely reacted in time, throwing ourselves to the ground as the furniture and walls exploded into splinters.

"They're going to tear us apart!" Billy shouted, gritting his teeth as he sought to find better cover.

—Keep your head down! —I replied, trying to find a way to counteract that infernal machine.

From his position, the Crow watched coldly as his gang cornered us with the Gatling gun. He knew he had the advantage. As the machine gun continued to fire, the outlaws advanced, covered by the hail of bullets. Some of them had already reached the bank facade, shooting through the broken windows.

The sheriff, crouched behind one of the counters, shouted instructions to his men, but the situation was desperate. Every shot we fired was answered by the Gatling gun with a torrent

of bullets that prevented us from moving.

"We have to do something or they're going to tear us apart," I said, tightening my grip on my gun as I looked at Billy.

"If we don't do anything, we won't get out of here alive," he replied, breathing heavily.

We knew we couldn't continue in that situation for much longer.

Then I saw something on the street that gave me an idea. One of the horses pulling the cart was starting to get nervous. The animal, agitated by the sound of the bullets and the chaos around it, was starting to pull hard on the reins. If I could shoot the rope holding the horses...

"Billy, cover my position," I shouted, and before he could answer, I was out of cover and up high enough to get a good view of the rope. The Gatling gun was focused in another direction, so I had only a second to act. I aimed carefully and fired.

The shot was accurate. The rope holding the horses broke and the cart overturned, throwing the machine gun to the ground.

—Nice shot! —Billy shouted, returning to his shooting position.

The sheriff and his men seized the moment. With the Gatling threat neutralized, we went back on the offensive. Bullets were flying everywhere, ricocheting off the walls and the

floor, and the Crow, seeing that things weren't going as he had planned, shouted an order to his men.

—Retreat! —his voice echoed above the din.

One by one, members of his band began to leap onto their horses and flee, firing as they retreated. The Raven was the last to leave, mounting his horse with an eerie calm. He glanced at us one last time before turning and riding with his band off into the horizon, disappearing into the dust kicked up by their hooves.

The Raven's Lair

The chase was long and exhausting. We had set out almost immediately, just after the Crow and his gang had retreated from the bank in the chaos. It was our only chance to catch him before he vanished again. The first few days of the chase were hard: we rode from dawn to dusk, following barely visible tracks through the dust and the mountains.

The nights were cold, and darkness seemed to cover everything with a blanket of impenetrable silence. We camped under the starry sky with our eyes fixed on the horizon, always alert in case the treacherous shadows of the Crow or one of his men approached. Fatigue began to weigh on our bodies, but determination did not let us stop.

"This damn Raven has a way of disappearing," Billy said one night as he stoked the camp fire.

"Yes, but he's leaving more tracks than he thinks," I replied, looking at the marks on the ground, traces of horse and boot tracks that indicated we were on the right track.

Finally, after several days of pursuit, we came to a place that seemed more gloomy and desolate than any other we had ever crossed. In the distance, a silhouette rose on the horizon: an old abandoned church, forgotten by time. The sun was beginning to set, casting long shadows on the dilapidated building. The wooden walls were rotten and covered with vines, and the crooked

bell tower seemed ready to fall. Could this be their hiding place?

"There they are," Billy said, nodding toward the church. In the distance, the Raven's horses and his men could be seen tied up near the ruins, grazing peacefully.

"We finally caught up with them," I said, a mixture of satisfaction and tension running through me. But we also knew that the hardest part was yet to come. If the Crow and his gang took refuge there, it would be difficult to confront them directly.

We approached cautiously, leaving our horses in a small grove of trees nearby, far enough away not to alert the outlaws. We crouched in the bushes, watching the movements of the Raven's men. There were at least five outside, posted like sentries, surveying the surroundings. They seemed relaxed, perhaps confident that no one had followed them to this forgotten corner of the world.

"What do we do now?" Billy asked in a whisper. I could sense his impatience, but also his concern.

"First, we have to make sure he's here. We can't let the Raven get away again," I said, scanning the terrain.

A couple of hours passed before anything else happened. Suddenly, the church doors opened and a figure emerged that could not be other than

Raven himself. His dark figure and the calm with which he moved gave him away. He seemed to be organizing his band, while pointing to the sentries and giving orders.

"There's the bastard," Billy muttered under his breath, his hand clenched on the handle of his revolver.

"Be patient," I warned him. "We'll wait until nightfall. Maybe we can get in and catch them by surprise."

The Raven disappeared back into the church, and one of the sentries began lighting a fire in front of the entrance. We knew we would have to move soon, but carefully. Night would fall quickly, and that would give us some advantage. But it also meant that if we weren't careful, we would be walking into a deadly trap.

"Let's get closer," I said to Billy, pointing to some rocks near the church where we could keep watch without being seen.

We moved stealthily, getting as close to the church as possible without attracting attention.

As I looked around the camp, an idea came to me. I knew that confronting them head-on would be suicide, but if we could separate them, we could catch the leader when he was alone.

"We need a distraction," I said quietly, turning to Billy.

Billy frowned thoughtfully. Suddenly, a sly smile spread across his face. "Dynamite," he

whispered, a gleam in his eyes.

— Dynamite?

—Yes. I have a couple of cartridges in my saddlebag. If I put a long-fuse one in that ravine a few yards away, the Raven's men will run over there. In the meantime, we go into the church and catch the Raven.

It was a risky plan, but we didn't have many other options.

Billy slipped over to where we had left the horses and returned with the dynamite. He went to the ravine and placed the dynamite carefully behind some rocks. He lit the fuse and returned within seconds, crouching beside me.

—Now, let's wait —he said.

The fuse moved forward slowly. A couple of minutes passed, which seemed like hours, until finally, the roar of the explosion shook the silence of the night. The sentries jumped up, confused, shouting among themselves.

—Let's go! —I said, quickly getting up and running towards the church.

Most of the Raven's men ran towards the site of the explosion, as we had anticipated. There were only two guards left at the gate, and we had no choice but to confront them. We rushed at them quickly, striking them before they could draw their weapons.

I pushed open the old church doors forcefully, the creaking of the rotten wood echoing in the

empty room. There was the Raven, sitting quietly on a bench, as if he had been waiting for us.

"I knew I'd see you again, Owen," she said with a smirk. "You were always so persistent."

We stared at each other, each sizing the other up, knowing this showdown had been years in the making.

"You won't get away this time," I said in a firm voice. Although I was sure the Crow had something planned, I couldn't trust him.

We pounced on him before he could react. At last, the man who had evaded justice so many times was at our mercy.

The Raven's Flight

The moon was rising over the desert as we began our journey back to Gold Valley. The silence between us and Raven, tied to his horse, was almost palpable. My mind replayed everything that had happened in the past few days. Raven, even with his hands bound, had not lost his defiant attitude. I wondered what was going through his mind as we rode toward our final destination, or so I thought at the moment.

—Are you sure you're going to bring me to justice? —He broke the silence with a voice that resonated with mockery—. Neither you nor that cheap sheriff will be able to keep me locked up.

I glanced at him, trying not to fall for his game. I knew him well, he was always looking for a way to sow doubt or fear, but I couldn't afford to hesitate anymore. We had caught him, and that was the end of him.

"You're going to pay for everything you've done," I replied without taking my eyes off the horizon.

—Pay? —The Raven let out a dry laugh. —This is just a small detour on my path. You know, Owen, deep down we are the same. You too have a past that you prefer to hide. How many times have you been on the other side of the law?

I didn't answer him. There was something about the way he spoke that unsettled me, an insidious calm that crept into my mind. But I

couldn't let his words get to me. What mattered now was to hand him over and put an end to this story.

When we reached Gold Valley, the little town was in the quiet of the night. The sheriff and his deputy watched us from the porch of their office. We pulled Crow off his horse, and Billy, with a triumphant smile, approached the sheriff.

"There you go, Sheriff," Billy said. "It wasn't easy, but we caught him eventually."

The sheriff eyed the Crow suspiciously. "This bastard has been a thorn in our side for too long," he said as he handcuffed him. "Good job, boys."

They took the Crow to a small cell, a simple iron structure that had been sufficient to hold other outlaws in the past. But something in the Crow's gaze, that insolent confidence, would not leave me alone.

"The judge will arrive in Gold Valley tomorrow morning," the sheriff said, closing the cell door with a loud bang.

I crossed my arms, watching as the Crow sat on the cot in the cell, as calm as if he were in his own home. I didn't say anything, but something told me this wasn't the end.

The next morning, I woke up to the sound of screaming in the street. I quickly stood up, adjusting my boots as I hurried out of my house. Billy was already outside, staring at the police

station with wide eyes.

— Owen! He's escaped! —he shouted, pointing towards the building.

The Raven had vanished. The cell doors were swung wide open, and the sheriff stood inside, cursing as he checked the broken chains.

—How the hell did he do this? —the sheriff asked, incredulously.

I walked towards the cell, my gaze scanning every detail, looking for some trace of how he had managed to escape. Then I saw it: on the bed, where the Raven had slept the night before, was a carefully folded note. I picked it up, instantly recognising the symbol of a black raven drawn on the paper. I opened the note and read the words written in neat but firm handwriting:

"Tonight, at 12, in the black canyon. Just you and me."

I felt a knot in my stomach. The Raven was challenging me, and I couldn't ignore it. He had escaped, but he wasn't hiding. He wanted to face me, face to face. I knew this wouldn't end any other way.

"What does the note say?" Billy asked, coming over to look over my shoulder.

I gave him the paper and as he read it, he frowned.

—That bastard... He wants you to go after him again. It's a trap, Owen. You know it.

I nodded silently. Sure it was a trap, but I had

no choice. The Raven wouldn't stop until one of us fell. And this time, the showdown wouldn't be with any intermediaries or distractions. It would be a duel, just like he wanted.

"Don't worry, Billy," I said, putting the note in my jacket. "This ends tonight."

Face to face

I knew I would have to face him alone. Billy, faithful as ever, insisted on accompanying me. But this time it was not to be.

"Billy, this is my fight," I said, my jaw clenched and my eyes fixed on the distance. "The Crow wants to see me. If you come, it could be worse."

—But you can't go alone, damn it! —He replied, his voice full of concern. —That man is a demon, and he won't be without his band.

I looked into his eyes, knowing he was right. But this was something I had to do alone.

—I know, Billy. But if I don't go, this won't end. It won't stop. And I won't risk it ending someone because of me.

Billy clenched his fists, but eventually he understood.

—If you don't come back before dawn, I'll follow you to the ends of the earth, Owen.

I patted him on the shoulder, grateful for his loyalty. Then I headed for my horse, a firm resolve in my heart. I knew this might be the end. But there was an unfinished debt between me and the Raven, one I couldn't leave unpaid.

Riding in the pale moonlight, the cold wind felt like blades against my skin. Each step of the horse echoed in the desolate terrain of the canyon, where shadows seemed to lengthen and twist like ghostly figures. The hills rose like dark

walls on either side, forming a narrow passage that led me straight to meet my destiny.

Finally, a clearing appeared before me. It was an open, flat space, surrounded by the high cliffs of the canyon. And there he was, right in the center, waiting for me like a predator stalking its prey. The Raven, wearing his trademark black hat, stood there, and he was not alone.

At least five of his men were with him, scattered in the shadows, their silhouettes barely visible in the moonlight.

"I knew you would come alone, Owen," the Raven said, his voice low but clear as a sharp blade.

My gaze scanned the area, searching for any chance to escape, but it was clear there was no easy way out. The Raven's men already had me surrounded.

—What I didn't expect —he continued, with a crooked smile—, is that you would be so predictable.

Before I could react, two of his men grabbed me from behind. I felt a blow to my head that made me dizzy, and before I knew it, I was tied to a chair in the middle of the clearing. The Raven sat in front of me with his piercing gaze fixed on mine.

"You thought you were done with me a long time ago, Owen," he said, leaning forward. "But you see, some of us come back from the dead."

My hands were tied tightly, but my mind kept searching for a way out. I looked at the men around him, all ready, hands near their weapons, waiting for the signal from their leader. But there was something about the way the Crow looked at me… he wasn't looking to kill me right away. He wanted something more.

—Why don't you just get it over with, Raven? —I replied, my voice full of contempt. —You've always been a coward, hiding behind your men. Now that you have the chance to finish me off, are you taking your time?

The Raven answered me with a coldness that gave me goosebumps.

—Because I don't want this to end quickly, Owen. I want to savor the moment. I want you to understand what it's like to lose everything, like I did.

He rose from his chair and walked slowly around me, his boots clicking on the dry canyon floor.

—Do you remember that day? —he asked, stopping right behind me. —The day you shot me and left me behind, abandoned me and left me for dead.

"That's a lie, although I should have finished you off," I replied angrily.

Suddenly, I felt the cold barrel of a revolver pressed against the back of my neck. The Crow had drawn his weapon and was holding it steady,

ready to fire.

"That's what I like most about you, Owen," he said, leaning toward me. "Always so direct. But what's your plan now? There's no one coming to save you this time."

I knew my time was running out. Billy wasn't here, and the situation seemed hopeless. But as the Crow threatened me, something in his tone told me he wasn't going to kill me yet. He liked the game. And that, perhaps, was my only redeeming feature.

"You've always been good at talking, Raven," I said calmly. "But in the end, you always lose. You know that."

The Crow laughed as he cocked his revolver and pressed it tighter to the back of my neck.

— Any last wish, Owen?

Duel in the clearing

The Raven barely had time to open his mouth when the distinctive sound of two rifles being loaded broke the silence of the night. The Raven and his men turned towards the sound, surprised.

"His wish is for you to let him go," said a firm, deep voice. I recognized that voice immediately.

From the shadows, Billy appeared with a rifle in each hand, aimed directly at the Crow's men. With sharp eyes and tight lips, he approached with determined steps, ready for whatever was coming.

The Raven growled in frustration, but waved his men to stop.

"Let him go," Billy said in a tone that left no room for argument.

One of the Crow's men reluctantly pulled out a knife and cut the ropes binding me. I rubbed my wrists as Billy tossed me one of my pistols.

"I knew you wouldn't leave me alone on this," I said with a half smile, gripping the handle of the revolver firmly.

"I wasn't going to let you die, Owen. Not today," Billy replied, still aiming at the outlaws.

The Raven looked at us with suppressed fury.
- Curse! -

Then, with a wave of his hand, the Raven's men stepped back, creating a semicircle around us. Silence fell again on the clearing, a heavy silence, broken only by the wind rustling through

the rocks.

"Owen," the Crow said, stepping forward, his hand already caressing the handle of his Colt. "Get ready. Nobody gets involved. This fight is between you and me."

We stood a few feet apart, staring each other in the eyes. The tension in the air was palpable. Every muscle in my body was tense, but my mind remained clear. I had known this moment would come since the day I saw him escape from the cell. This duel was inevitable.

"Billy," I said quietly, not taking my eyes off the Crow. "Stay out of this. This is my business."

Billy, still holding his weapons at the ready, nodded and stepped back. I knew he would respect my decision, though his concern was evident in his eyes.

The moonlight illuminated the clearing, creating long shadows and marking the ground as if it were a stage set for a duel to the death. The Raven watched me with a cold, cruel smile, his hat tilted slightly forward, obscuring part of his face.

"I thought you wouldn't have the courage to face me," said the Raven, his deep voice cutting through the silence like a razor. "But I guess patience has paid off. Today is the day it all ends."

"Yes, it ends today," I replied, not letting the fear show in my voice.

We were both ready. In the distance, the sound of crickets and the wind were the only witnesses of what was about to happen. I positioned myself in the center of the clearing with my hand near the revolver. The Crow did the same with his gaze fixed on me, waiting for the exact moment.

Time seemed to stand still. I felt my heart pounding in my chest, but my mind remained calm, focused. Everything came down to that moment. The tension increased with each passing second, until words became unnecessary.

In an instant, we both moved. The sound of leather as I pulled out my revolver was barely audible, overshadowed by the roar of the gunshots that rent the air. My Colt was firm in my hand, and I pulled the trigger without hesitation.

The first shot rang out like thunder. I saw the spark from the Crow's revolver just before I felt the impact in my side. A sharp burn went through me, but my shot had also found its mark. The Crow faltered, a look of surprise on his face. He staggered back, bringing his hand to his chest, where a red stain began to rapidly expand.

Silence returned to the clearing. The Raven fell to his knees, his revolver falling from his hand to the ground with a dull thud. His men, who had been watching expectantly, did not move. They knew their leader had lost.

I walked towards him, one hand on the wound in my side, feeling the blood soaking through my shirt. Every step hurt, but I couldn't stop.

The Raven looked at me, a mixture of hatred and resignation in his eyes. He coughed, spitting blood, and tried to speak.

—I'll see you in hell, Owen—she murmured—

I stopped in front of him with my revolver still in my hand, pointing down.

"I'll make sure you leave, Raven," I said firmly, though fatigue was creeping in.

The Raven smiled at me one last time with a bitter and defeated look. His body fell to the ground, motionless, as blood slowly spread across the ground.

Billy ran to me, his face full of worry. I leaned on him as the adrenaline began to fade and the pain in my side intensified.

"You did it, Owen," Billy said, his tone a mixture of relief and admiration. "You did it."

The last flight of the Raven

Suddenly, in the distance, the sound of hooves broke the silence. The shadows of horsemen emerged on the horizon, moving quickly towards the clearing. The brightness of the stars was unmistakable. It was the sheriff and his deputies.

I knew Billy hadn't come alone. A few minutes before the confrontation, Billy had sent a boy from the village with a note, explaining the situation and asking for reinforcements. I never thought they would arrive just in time, but there they were, ready to clean up the mess left behind by the Crow's death.

The Raven's men, seeing their leader lying lifeless on the ground, stood still.

Their looks, which had previously been ones of contempt and defiance, turned to pure surrender. The sheriff didn't have to say much. He barely raised a hand, and his deputies drew their weapons, aiming them at the outlaws. With the tension broken and the certainty that it was all over, the Raven's henchmen dropped their weapons one by one, throwing them to the ground with a hollow sound.

"No one else has to die," the sheriff growled, dismounting with a gesture of authority. His voice echoed like a final sentence in the clearing. "Kneel and raise your arms."

The men obeyed without question. The sheriff's face was hard, but there was some relief

in his eyes when he saw me standing, wounded, but still breathing. Blood was still flowing from my side, but in my mind, all was calm. The Raven was no longer a threat, and that was all that mattered at that moment.

"You did good, Owen," the sheriff said, patting me on the shoulder as one of his deputies handcuffed the Raven's men.

He turned to them and ordered.

—Take them to town. We're going to make sure these guys spend a long time in a cell. And that no one ever hears anything about the Crow again.

We slowly mounted our horses and headed back to the village. Every step my horse took made the pain in my side throb harder, but I stood my ground. I wasn't going to give in after everything I'd been through.

When we reached Gold Valley, the stillness of the night contrasted with the intensity of the fighting. We made our way to Dr. Taylor's house. As we entered, the dim light of the oil lamps illuminated the place, giving it a warm, welcoming air that almost made us forget the dangers we had left behind in the canyon.

"Let me see that wound, Owen," the doctor said in a worried tone when he saw me.

They helped me into a chair as I removed my bloody shirt. The doctor worked silently, cleaning and stitching the wound. I felt each

stitch burn, but I kept my gaze fixed on the window, where the moon shone brightly overhead, a silent witness to everything that had happened.

Billy stood beside me, not saying much. I knew words were unnecessary at that moment. We had both been through too much and understood that this chapter of our story was coming to an end. But there was a sense in the air that new storms were brewing.

"That's it, Owen," the doctor said, covering the wound with a clean bandage. "You'll need to rest for a few days, but you'll be fine."

"Thanks, Doc," I replied with a slight nod.

I sat back in my chair a little, letting exhaustion take over as Billy and the doctor talked. In my mind, I couldn't help but remember what had happened: the confrontation with the Crow. It had all happened so fast, but at the same time, every moment seemed etched in my memory.

As I let my body begin to relax, the moonlight, brighter now, cast shadows across the window. Looking up, a peculiar silhouette appeared on the ground, right in front of me. The shadow seemed to take the form of a raven spreading its wings. I stared at the image, caught up in the symbolism. It was as if the very spirit of the Raven was still there, watching over me from somewhere beyond.

That raven drawn by the moon on the wooden

floor was a silent reminder that, although he had fallen, his name would remain a legend in the West. It was the Raven's last flight.

The night became quieter as I finally gave in to exhaustion. As I closed my eyes, that crow-like silhouette projected on the ground slowly faded away, as if it were flying in search of new shadows. I thought about what was to come, about what was yet to happen.

Because, as always, the dawn would bring with it new challenges and we would be ready to face any challenge.

Venture into the barren lands of the Old West with Owen Stone and his young sidekick Billy!

Don't miss their exciting adventures and continue with VOLUME 2

The legend of Owen Stone awaits you!